Hearts and Heirs:

Charlotte and Nathaniel

(Book 1)

Sophia Blakely

© Copyright by Sara Blakely 2024 - All rights reserved.

The content contained within this book may not be reproduced, duplicated or transmitted without direct written permission from the author or the publisher.

Under no circumstances will any blame or legal responsibility be held against the publisher, or author, for any damages, reparation, or monetary loss due to the information contained within this book. Either directly or indirectly. You are responsible for your own choices, actions, and results.

Legal Notice:

This book is copyright protected. This book is only for personal use. You cannot amend, distribute, sell, use, quote or paraphrase any part, or the content within this book, without the consent of the author or publisher.

Disclaimer Notice:

Please note the information contained within this document is for educational and entertainment purposes only. All effort has been executed to present accurate, up to date, and reliable, complete information. No warranties of any kind are declared or implied. Readers acknowledge that the author is not engaging in the rendering of legal, financial, medical or professional advice. The content within this book has been derived from various sources. Please consult a licensed professional before attempting any techniques outlined in this book.

By reading this document, the reader agrees that under no circumstances is the author responsible for any losses, direct or indirect, which are incurred as a result of the use of the information contained within this document, including, but not limited to, — errors, omissions, or inaccuracies.

Table Of Contents

Chapter 1 4

Chapter 2 12

Chapter 3 20

Chapter 4 28

Chapter 5 36

Chapter 6 47

Chapter 7 57

Chapter 8 66

Chapter 9 75

Chapter 10 83

Chapter 11 93

Chapter 12 102

Chapter 13 111

Chapter 14 121

Chapter 15 133

Chapter 16 142

Chapter 17 151

Chapter 18 161

Chapter 19 171

Chapter 20 178

Chapter 21 190

Epilogue 200

Chapter 1

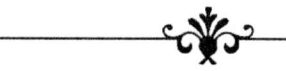

The grand manor stood silent; its walls cloaked in the weight of history. Secrets whispered through the corridors like restless ghosts, their voices echoing in the stillness, their stories woven into the very fabric of the manor.

Charlotte Green—Lottie—was only 12 when she entered the house and service through double oak doors almost three times her height. She knew every creaky floorboard and every draughty windowpane, but she knew very little of those whispered secrets. She knew only the stories told to her by the white-haired elderly mistress of Ringwood Manor, and sometimes those seemed like fairy tales.

Lady Eleanor Gilroy, a former shining star of London's glittering balls, lay still in the centre of her four-poster bed. Her mind, once as sharp as a rapier, had dulled, and her body, once the envy of society, now bore the weariness of countless seasons.

In the dim glow of a single candle, Lady Eleanor stirred. Her blue eyes, clouded by the mists of memory, drifted unseeing over the once familiar contours of her chamber. The bed where she became a woman, bore no children, but mourned their loss in the dead of the night, and said farewell to the love of her life, her husband.

The devoted maid who had tended to Lady Eleanor for the past five years, kept vigil by her mistress's side. She had forsaken her own bed, choosing instead to rest in a creaking wooden chair, her eyes never leaving the frail form before her.

Lottie took her place as darkness fell, as she had for the past five nights; she dragged the rocking chair, resting its curved feet against the bed, and took the Lady's hand.

She told her what she had been up to during the day, the story always the same. Rise at dawn, light the fires, sweep the walkways, launder the Lady's clothes and linens, run errands, church on Sunday, Wednesday afternoon off.

Lottie's voice seemed to calm her mistress, stilled the fidgeting of restless fingers, plucking at the linen sheets covering her, occasionally gripping an invisible needle, sewing non-existent stitches into samplers from a time gone by.

The doorbell rang loudly, startling both Lottie and her mistress, whose cloudy eyes opened, grey as a storm-battered sky on a summer's day.

"Lottie," Lady Eleanor rasped, as if the words scraped and scratched on their way out of her mouth. "The crows are coming."

She lifted her clawed hand and pointed toward the window, where the winter moonlight shone through the gap in the curtains. Lottie stood, pulled the edges of the heavy-lined velvet together, and returned to the bed.

"Milady, I am here. Please rest."

As a maid, her hands were rough from manual work but salved nightly at Lady Eleanor's insistence with a generous slathering of the Lady's favourite hand cream, a habit her mistress instilled in her years ago. She took the greatest care, making gentle movements as she smoothed the sheets around her mistress, plumped the pillows, offering what comfort she could, but it never felt enough.

Lottie smoothed that same hand cream on the translucent skin of Lady Eleanor's hands now and rubbed her own hands together to absorb the excess before returning the lid to the heavy glass jar that sat on the table at the bedside.

"Stealing before my dear sister-in-law has even departed this world?" A harsh nasal voice, accompanied by the rustle and swish of silk, caused Lottie to turn.

An angular lady dressed in black silk, with a heavy black shawl embroidered with colourful flowers across her shoulders, bonnet still in place, stood in the doorway and looked down her sharp nose in disdain.

Lottie stood and bobbed a curtsy to the stranger, who entered the room without knocking.

The lady looked about the room, wrinkled her nose, and sniffed with distaste before covering her nose with a handkerchief. Lottie took offence at the lady's reaction, knowing the room was spotless, scented with fresh snowdrops picked from the manor's garden first thing that morning, and her mistress's favourite scent.

"Madam." Lottie's tone was curt as she stepped forward, about to issue a rebuke to this interloper, when Holmes, the houseman, rapped on the doorframe.

"Lady Anne, your chamber is ready. If you'll follow me, I have a maid to help you unpack." His words were polite but held no warmth.

Lady Anne? Lottie did not recognise the name from any of Lady Eleanor's stories, but she must have heard about the mistress's demise and come to Ringwood to pay her respects. Possibly the first of many visitors, as was customary, at times such as these, Holmes had explained this to Lottie a few days before.

If they are all as rude as Lady Anne, maybe it would be better if they never came at all.

***

Another visitor arrived as Lady Anne sat at the head of the table in the formal dining room, rarely used since the mistress's health deteriorated. Lottie peered around the door as she came down to the kitchen to refresh the water pitcher.

"Mr. Forbes, milady's solicitor. Dr. Bamber advised we call for one, after he examined milady this morning," Maggie, the cook, advised, as she nudged the girl away with her hip, bringing a plate of food through to the latest arrival.

"He barely looks old enough," Lottie said, as Maggie returned with Lady Anne's empty plate and dish.

"And sulking like a child to boot." Maggie shook her head. "Whining about having to leave a lucrative card game in Winchester."

Both looked up as Holmes, Maggie's husband, came into the kitchen.

"Lottie, milady is fretting for you."

Lottie picked up the pitcher of water and hurried up the back stairs to her mistress's chamber, entering the room silently.

Lady Eleanor muttered in the space between waking and dreaming, and she spoke of Miss Amelia—the daughter of the Lady's late brother—her words often indistinct, her voice filled with melancholy and regret.

Lottie knew of Miss Amelia only through a faded portrait that hung in the hallway, a young girl with eyes that mirrored Lady Eleanor's own, pale blue and wide, as if surprised by the world.

The portrait was a window into the past, a glimpse of a life that had once been part of the manor's tapestry.

Lady Eleanor twisted her head, her cloudy eyes searching for something unseen, before her gaze fell on her maid.

"Milord's study, the desk drawer... my will." The woman pulled weakly on Lottie's hand, and the girl leaned forward to hear the urgency in the whispered words. "Behind the secret panel."

Lottie nodded, her heart fluttering with a mix of duty and curiosity. She turned to go, but her mistress's gnarled hand grasped hers tightly for a second. As the Lady slipped back to slumber, her hand dropped gently to her side.

The girl slipped through the dimly lit corridor, stepping carefully to avoid the noisy floorboards so as not to wake their visitors, who may have retired for the evening. When Lottie turned the corner, where the study was the last room on the left, a flicker of candlelight spilled into the hallway.

The door was ajar, and a figure hunched over the vast leather-topped desk. Lottie held her breath, so as not to give away her presence, listening to the rustle of papers.

She gasped as she recognised the sharp features of Lady Anne and knocked on the door softly, interrupting the nighttime search.

Lady Anne straightened, lifting the candle, her gaze piercing. Lottie's eyes fell upon a pile of envelopes on the desk's surface.

"Are you looking for something, milady—" Lottie stepped into the room, pausing for a moment, aware of the significance of this room.

The study's oak-panelled walls were lined with well-thumbed leather-bound volumes and ink-stained quills. It was a sanctuary of knowledge, a repository of wisdom, a testament to Lady Eleanor's love of reading before her eyesight failed, and her concentration waned years since.

"—for something to read?" Lottie finished, as she stood by the desk.

Lady Anne's gaze narrowed, peeved to have been discovered.

"Indeed, my girl. The journey from Bath is long, and I am tired, but I always like to read before I retire." She reached out to select a book, without so much as looking at the title, and Lottie knew she did not speak the truth.

Lottie bowed her head as the woman exited, waiting for the light from her candle to disappear before she executed her instructions.

The envelopes, addressed to Lady Eleanor in a flowing hand, were still sealed, and Lottie's curiosity battled briefly with loyalty, then she tucked the letters into her apron, better to keep them undisturbed on her person than risk the return of Lady Anne.

Lottie's duty was clear, to retrieve the will and nothing more. The unread words and secrets locked within parchment folds would stay thus. The girl opened the first of three drawers, filled only with paper and envelopes. The second held bric-a-brac, which she pushed aside, and reached for the back of the drawer, pushing firmly. There was some movement, and Lottie pushed harder.

A secret drawer popped forward, and there, in the light of the candle, a yellowed document, sealed with wax lay there. She cradled it like a fragile bird, in both hands, blowing out the candle as she left the study.

As she returned to Lady Eleanor's chamber, there was an audience already gathered. Lady Anne glared, Forbes stifled a yawn, and Holmes, the loyal servant he was, stood with his head bowed in silent communion.

Lottie held her breath as she approached the bed. Milady was so still that she wondered if she had already left this world before she could say goodbye.

Lady Eleanor's eyes fluttered open, and for a fleeting moment, clarity returned, or at least it seemed. She smiled, her hands reaching out to Lottie.

"Amelia, darling girl," she whispered, "you are home."

Lottie's heart swelled with both sadness and love. She knelt, pressing her lips to the back of one of the Lady's hands, and pressed the document into the other.

"My Lady Eleanor," Lottie whispered.

The old lady's silver hair spilled across the pillow, a halo of memories, and Lottie thought her mistress looked like an angel, as she drew her last breath.

In that quiet room, amidst the echoes of a grand manor, Lottie became the keeper of the unread letters in her pocket. As the clock struck the late hour, the Manor bid a silent welcome to a new era, its walls echoing with the whispers of the past and an undiscovered future.

Chapter 2

The flickering candle in Lady Eleanor's chamber cast elongated shadows on the walls, and the air thickened with anticipation. Lottie remained by her mistress's side, her vigil unyielding, even as Lady Anne and Forbes silently retired to their quarters.

Holmes, the houseman, lingered in the hallway, making sure the guests were securely ensconced in their rooms. His stern countenance softened as he re-entered the bedroom, his eyes falling on Lottie.

It had been five years since he had found her in a tavern in Winchester, where a group of men were taking bets on which of them could tame the 'wild wench' who worked as a pot girl in the Royal Oak. She had grown into a fine young woman, with the guidance of both Maggie, his wife, and her Ladyship.

Lottie, still overcome with emotion, forgot herself for a moment and used her apron to wipe the tears from her face. As she stood, ready to attend to Lady Eleanor's body, Holmes reached out and rested his hand on her shoulder.

His voice, gravelly and low, carried a weight of authority.

"Wait," he said. "I've sent for Maggie; she'll help with the mistress."

"But— "

Lottie's eyes widened. Her duty was clear—to care for Lady Eleanor—but over the past weeks, as the old lady's breaths had grown shallower, her role had blurred.

She had become more than a maid; she was a comfort in the Lady's hour of need, a counsel when she cried out in the night.

Maggie arrived, her apron dusted with flour, for although the house was shrouded in death, life went on, along with mouths to feed on the morrow.

"Your duty is done, milady," Holmes whispered, as he covered his mistress's face with a sheet. "Rest now."

Lottie's tears welled up, blurring her vision.

"Your duty is done too, my duck," Maggie cooed, as she hugged Lottie. "Go to bed. We've a busy time ahead."

Heavy of heart and tired of limb, Lottie moved slowly along the corridor to the stairs that would take her to her room in the attic. At the end, where she should turn left, she paused, her hands finding the envelopes in her apron pocket. The study beckoned, that sanctuary of secrets.

She should take them back to where they belonged, for they were not hers to hold. But she did not know where Lady Anne had found them, and she did not want to leave them again on the top of the desk, in case the woman went in search of them. If Lady Eleanor had never opened the letters addressed to her, had never read them, her sister-in-law had no need to know what was contained within.

In her attic room, Lottie tossed and turned in her bed, her mind furiously running around in circles about what was next for her. She knew she needed to do her duty as ever in the coming days, but what of the next weeks, months, what future waited for her?

Lottie squeezed her eyes shut, determined to fall into the blackness of sleep. But like the siren song heard by sailors lost at sea, Lottie was called by the secrets sealed in parchment hidden under her pillow. She drifted off, exhausted, but her mind was not ready to surrender.

She had never once been deceitful to her mistress, but now, with Lady Anne's timely arrival at her sister-in-law's bedside just in time for her passing, Lottie wondered what had drawn the woman to Ringwood Manor.

Just one letter to find out who the sender was. I'll read no more than their name.

There were 15 letters, all in the same hand, so someone had something important to say to Lady Eleanor. Why had her mistress never opened them? Was it someone she no longer wished to know of, hence putting the missives out of sight and out of mind? What if it were Lady Anne who wrote some incriminatory words and that was why she searched them out?

The candle at her bedside sputtered out as if some force worked unseen. A shiver passed along Lottie's skin, not in fear, but in anticipation of excitement, of the unknown, of possible adventure.

In the years of service to Lady Eleanor, she learned life could be calm and consistent. She was safe and secure at Ringwood Manor. Although she clearly remembered her life before, she tucked it away deep inside and not even Holmes and Maggie knew fully of the despair of her childhood. A mother who earned her money on her back, a father whose name she never knew. Life had been hard, and she survived by dreaming about what might have been instead of what was.

She would never go back to that life again, but she could not continue without a mistress. Perhaps the letters might provide some information about Lady Anne and her link to Lady Eleanor. Provide something that would help Lottie decide on her future.

Lottie got out of bed, pulled a blanket around her, and sat in front of the embers of the fire, which she stoked back to a flame. She took a deep breath, carefully opened an envelope and the aged paper inside, and she started to read.

The letter spoke of love and respect for Lady Eleanor and an apology for an unnamed betrayal. Miss Amelia Colton's hand signed her name in large looping letters at the end of the single page and Lottie's heart raced as she opened another.

She pieced together fragments—an estranged niece, her secret love, and a grieving aunt who never knew the truth. Along with the will that Lady Eleanor bid her fetch, but did not get to read before she took her final breath, there was a mystery of which Lottie was the only one aware.

As dawn painted the sky, Lottie's eyes grew heavy. She lay down on her bed, the letters clutched to her heart. The truth as yet eluded her, and her conscience prevented her from reading more than two. But she vowed to uncover it so that she might understand what Lady Eleanor's legacy would mean for her niece, Amelia.

The young lady clearly cared enough to write so many times, even though she likely received no answer. Amelia might have thought that her aunt no longer loved her, but Lady Eleanor's words disproved that.

Lottie knew she would discover the truth, and she would make sure Amelia discovered it too.

***

The next morning, Forbes descended the stairs, his disapproval etched into every crease of his suit. He had been kept awake by the old house settling into its first night without its mistress.

He sat heavily in his seat to the right-hand side of Lady Anne at the head of the table and barked at the servant who came through the door from the kitchen.

"Bring me coffee."

Lottie, tired herself, gritted her teeth, and carefully poured coffee into one of Lady Eleanor's elegant china cups. Forbes splashed cream on top and slurped the hot liquid, without so much as acknowledging her presence.

After two cups, and a plate of sausage, bacon, and eggs, he recovered enough spirit to recognise the deceased niece as she came to clear his plate.

"Everyone is here, capital," Forbes smiled widely and reached for the leather folder on the table beside him. "Shall we read Lady Gilroy's will?"

Lottie gasped, even as a servant, she knew how inappropriate Mr. Forbes' suggestion was. She disappeared back into the kitchen and tried to catch her breath.

Lady Anne cast the young solicitor a long look, her eyes flinty.

"Bad form, Mr. Forbes," she declared.

In the kitchen, Lottie's lethargy weighed upon her, shadows pooling beneath her eyes. The truth of her situation, of the loss of her beloved mistress, writ large in the solicitor's mention of the will.

Holmes stepped forward, concern etching his features.

"Lottie," he said, "remove your apron. Go back to bed. You need rest."

Lottie removed her apron and headed out to the hallway, towards the back stairs. As she set her foot on the first step, the solicitor appeared through the kitchen door, closely followed by Holmes.

"I apologise, madam," the solicitor called out, his voice softer. "My deepest sympathies for your loss."

Lottie turned as the man's gaze fell upon her, and she saw a mixture of pity—which she had seen on many people's faces before, back in her childhood— and something else. Something she did not recognise.

His words rendered Lottie speechless, and she lowered her head, tears threatening to fall, and it wasn't her place, as a servant, to show emotion. Why was he apologising to her?

"We haven't been formally introduced, Miss Colton. I am Joseph Forbes, representative of your late aunt's solicitor."

He bowed courteously, and as he did so, Lottie looked to Holmes, her eyes wide in confusion. Lady Anne exited the dining room into the hallway and watched the scene unfolding, her eyes beady. Lottie waited for her to screech loudly at the man's mistake, but she did not utter a word.

The solicitor waited for Holmes to complete the introductions, as was customary in society, where a young lady could not initiate a conversation without these formalities. In lieu of a male relative, or indeed any relation at all, the onus fell to the houseman.

"Miss Amelia Colton," Holmes started to say, and his gaze, along with Lottie's and Lady Anne's moved to the portrait of the real Amelia on the wall to the left of where the solicitor stood.

Forbes followed suit and seemed to see enough of a likeness between a young Amelia and Lottie standing before him. True enough, the dark hair and light eyes were similar enough. He stepped forward and bowed once more.

Lottie, holding her apron wadded in her hands behind her back, inclined her head just a little, and pressed her lips together hard. Forbes nodded kindly, as if acknowledging she was too overcome with emotion to speak.

"I will return for Lady Gilroy's funeral, once arranged. I'll wait for your instructions on the details from your man. Good day, Miss Colton."

Lady Anne, ever watchful, insisted on seeing him out, and Lottie took the opportunity to head to her room. She had not the wit or capacity to deal with what had just unfolded and trusted that Holmes would provide guidance, as he had before, as she learned to negotiate her role as maid to a grand lady.

The grand manor held its breath once more as she climbed the stairs to her room, its walls echoing with whispered promises and unspoken truths.

Chapter 3

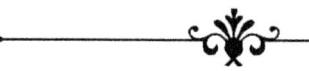

Lord Nathaniel Audley-Sinclair, Earl of Bevanbrook, stood in the dimly lit study on the first floor of his London townhouse; its location chosen because of the excellent view it gave of the street in both directions.

His profession made it necessary, at times, to pay close attention to who may be approaching his house at all hours of the day or night. Such was the private nature of his business. His clients, if they chose to attend his property, were careful to conceal their identity as well as their agenda.

The nature of his personal activities often required a quick getaway, for himself or for the female company he kept. Just two days since, a righteously determined fiancé of a female acquaintance of Nathaniel's made a somewhat wobbly approach up the centre of the road, brandishing a sword, seemingly willing to fight to the death for his beloved's honour.

Nathaniel had no concern about that particular young man, who had no military experience to speak of, certainly nothing to compare with the battles the Lord had experienced in the Napoleonic wars. The young man in question had taken one look at Nathaniel, backlit by several dozen candles, as he stood in the bay window of the study, his shirt tails untucked, brandishing two pistols. The would-be aggressor turned tail and fled in a much straighter line than when he approached, and left Nathaniel amused because the pistols were purely decorative.

This evening, the flicker of a single candle danced upon the mahogany desk, casting elongated shadows across the polished floor. Tonight, he was dining with his closest friend, Barnaby, Earl of Freshford, at their favourite gentlemen's club. His friend had been out of town for some months, both on business and spending time at his fiancée's family home.

Nathaniel was happy for Barnaby, who was besotted by Miss Daniella Hayes. She was a pleasant enough girl, intelligent, talented, with a dry sense of humour. There was no doubt that the girl had done very well in securing Barnaby's affections, and she seemed to care for him very much. Nathaniel had dealings with the girl's father, in his capacity as Judge, and if he had been in the business of marriage, one of the four Hayes daughters would make sense. But his friend had the best of the bunch, and Nathaniel had no intention of becoming anyone's husband.

Looking out the window now, waiting for Barnaby's carriage to arrive, Nathaniel saw a boy approach, stopping under a gas light to check the address on an envelope he pulled from his satchel. The boy approached the house, and Nathaniel heard the bell; his manservant brought the letter to his master.

Nathaniel traced the embossed red wax seal on the letter in his hands as he crossed the room and took a seat, not at his desk, but in the armchair in front of the fire. The manila envelope bore the stamp of Lightfoot and Geary Solicitor, a missive that no doubt bore sombre tidings.

The wax, further evidence of the seriousness of the message, yielded to his touch, revealing the elegant script within on headed paper. He was already acquainted with the London office of Lightfoot and Geary, having personal business with them some years before, and as he saw the subject of the letter, the words blurred momentarily as he made the connection. Something, he hoped, that the Winchester office, from whence the news originated, had not made.

The sender regretfully informed Lord Audley-Sinclair of the sorrowful news of the passing of Lady Eleanor Gilroy, widow of the Lord Allington Gilroy, belated of Ringwood Manor, Hampshire. The funeral would be held at the Manor two days hence, at midday.

Nathaniel stroked his chin as he pondered his quandary. He had previous plans in two days hence, which demanded his presence—a clandestine rendezvous with Molly Benning-Doyle, the vivacious red-headed beauty from Belgravia. She was a married woman, of course, but her allure had a way of erasing moral boundaries. Besides, he was far too impatient to invest time and energy into courting a woman of his own. Married women already knew what they liked and did not require wooing and winning over. The fact they required very little apart from his undivided attention for however long he was willing to give it, pleased him no end.

Yet, the death of Lady Eleanor Gilroy meant duty called louder than desire. Nathaniel's late mother had been a confidante of Lady Eleanor, and now, as the last of the Gilroy line succumbed to old age, he must pay his respects.

It had been some years since Lady Eleanor had retreated to the country estate permanently after Lord Gilroy's death, leaving behind the high society of London for the quietude of Hampshire. Nathaniel recalled her grace and wit on the occasions he had accompanied his mother as a youth and, in later years, her support when his mother had taken ill after a fall from her horse.

He recalled with more clarity the deeper connection between their two families that Lady Gilroy was unaware of, a secret he held close to his chest. Only he and one other knew the truth, and he was the sole guardian of that secret. For him, it was more than a matter of duty, he owed it to one of the very few people he loved in this world. The very least he could do in honour of their memory.

***

The graveside service was a muted affair. A handful of elderly people gathered—former friends from a generation that had lost touch with Lady Eleanor when she withdrew to the countryside were not in attendance. These were the country set, who had known only one version of the great lady. They whispered their goodbyes among themselves, their faces etched with the lines of time, their group growing smaller with every passing year.

Nathaniel observed them from a respectful distance, his gaze lingering on the two other small groups of mourners, an elderly woman and a young, suited man, and what appeared to be the household staff. Lady Eleanor's houseman stood still, his shoulders straight, looking straight ahead, like a pillar of stoicism. Nathaniel recognised him from his visits to Ringwood—the man who tended to the estate's every need, but also as a former military man.

Between the houseman and a comely grey-haired woman in a neat grey dress, stood a woman veiled in mourning. Her posture was rigid, her grief palpable from the quiet sobs that escaped from under the thick black veil and the whiteness of her knuckles as she gripped the hand of the other woman. Nathaniel wondered about her—perhaps a distant relative or a devoted servant.

Her attire caught his attention. The widow's weeds clung to her like a shroud, their cut and fabric reminiscent of a bygone era. Lady Eleanor's remnants, he assumed, handed down to a deserving servant.

The tears probably had more to do with self-pity and uncertainty about the maid's future, rather than genuine sorrow at the passing of their mistress.

Life and personal experience had made him cynical. His own servants were handpicked for their loyalty and their discretion; he had his own secrets he preferred to keep that way, and his staff were an extension of his presence in society. They were well paid, well fed and watered, well clothed, and had comfortable accommodations, particularly those involving personal contact with himself and those in his inner circle.

The vicar's voice rose in prayer, bringing Nathaniel's attention back to the reason for his presence. He bowed his head, paying the homage due to a Lady.

Nathaniel was an observer—a connoisseur of human intricacies. The crowd shifted once the vicar finished the committal, and he indulged in his other favourite pastime: watching people. The elderly mourners approached the household staff and shared their condolences. One by one, they stopped before the woman in black, shaking her hand, nodding their heads, their expressions a blend of sympathy and curiosity. Yet Nathaniel had no clue of her identity.

The air smelled of damp earth and freshly turned soil—a scent that clung to memories and whispered of final farewells. In turn, Nathaniel joined the queue, and he overheard the murmurs—a niece, they said. Lady Eleanor's niece. This puzzled him greatly. Lady Eleanor's niece had been estranged for years, but he had never heard any talk of her, at any salon or gathering he had joined. This niece must be from Lord Gilroy's side of the family, there was no other explanation.

As he neared the front, the introductions unfolded. The young man who stood now beside the young woman, in place of the houseman seemed to shrink under Nathaniel's scrutiny and cleared his throat as Nathaniel reached the front. The man's eyes darted nervously, as if seeking escape. Nathaniel was accustomed to other men feeling inadequate in his presence, but this wasn't what bothered him.

His gaze shifted to the woman. Even up close, the thick veil was impenetrable. Nathaniel adopted a polite expression, waiting for the formalities. The silence stretched, and then a hand settled on his forearm. He turned to find an older lady at his side, her veil more fashionable, less oppressive.

"My Lord, if you'll permit me."

Nathaniel inclined his head but was at a loss as to the older woman's name. She held herself well and was likely to be within Lady Eleanor's peers, so he made a best guess.

"Thank you, my Lady."

She rewarded him with a smile.

"May I present Lady Eleanor's..." she paused long enough to create tension, and Nathaniel caught a sharp intake of breath from the woman behind the veil. "Estranged niece, Miss Amelia Colton. Amelia, this is Lord Nathaniel Audley-Sinclair."

The words hung in the air, laden with drama. Nathaniel took Miss Colton's barely proffered gloved hand, and pressed his lips, his eyes never leaving hers.

There was a wry twist to his lips as he spoke her name.

"Miss Colton."

Amelia.

The weight of her grief seeped through the fabric, and he held her hand a beat longer than propriety dictated.

Her emotion seemed genuine, but there was no discerning her face. What lay hidden under the veil? Sorrow? Resentment? The truth? He could not tell, not without seeing the whites of her eyes.

"I'm sincerely sorry for your loss," he murmured, the words far more calculated than genuine.

He stalked away, leaving Miss Amelia Colton behind. Unexpected concern gnawed at him. Nathaniel knew one version of the truth about what happened to Lady Eleanor's niece. He would be very, very interested to find out what version of the truth *Amelia* would share, from behind the shadow of her veil.

Chapter 4

Since the reading of the will, the same afternoon as the funeral, Lady Anne, a tyrant in mourning attire, rattled through Ringwood Manor like a storm. Her footsteps echoed off the walls, each thud a proclamation of ownership. Lottie, comfortable in her role of the unassuming maid, knew her place—out of Lady Anne's path, out of her wrath.

Mr. Forbes outlined that everything contained within the Ringwood Estate and all other investments left to Lady Gilroy following her husband's death should pass to her niece, Amelia Colton. The household staff, from houseman to housemaid, would be retained until such time they secured alternative employment, retired or married, with a generous loyalty payment held in trust.

Lottie, overcome with emotion and gratitude at the immediate security of her future, was unable to speak during the reading and sat with bowed head. Lady Anne was not even mentioned in the will and radiated bitter but silent disappointment.

Mr. Forbes offered Lottie his condolences once more as he left the house, reminding her that he would be at her service whenever she needed him, be that the drafting of her own will or any other legal matters.

As soon as the young solicitor left, Lady Anne's tongue was as sharp as the silverware Lottie polished. Cruel comments dripped from her lips, accusing Lottie of deception.

"Besmirching Lady Eleanor's memory." Lady Anne's eyes bore into Lottie's, icy and unforgiving. "Pretending to be her precious niece."

And day after day, Lottie's heart clenched tighter and tighter. She longed to tell the woman that she had fed into the lie. What did she mean by introducing her to that Lord as Miss Amelia Colton? Not once had Lottie voiced the words to transform herself into Lady Eleanor's niece.

She wanted to tell her that she was not welcome here. If Lottie ever had any intention of assuming another's identity, she would take great pleasure in delivering that message to the woman, who seemed bent on outstaying her welcome, if she was ever welcome at all.

As Lottie, the humble servant, she had a job as long as she wanted it at Ringwood Manor, but without any mistress, without Lady Eleanor, there seemed little point. She had no intention of being subordinate to Lady Anne.

As Amelia, the heir to the Gilroy estate, she could ascend to heights she had only dreamed of as a child.

While her mother went about her business, young Lottie, in her only dirty ragged dress, used to watch the rich ladies as they walked and talked through the green parks. They were clean, shiny, and pretty, their hair piled high with ribbons and bows, wearing beautiful colours of pink, blue, and yellow. Lottie was dirty, her dress grey, her hair matted.

But she would not voice the past nor her dreams of an impossible future, especially not to Lady Anne.

One day, a week after the funeral, Lady Anne cornered her in the corridor. Her voice, low and sibilant, sliced through the air.

"You played your part well," she whispered. "I see that out of love and respect for my beloved sister-in-law, you pretended to be Amelia. To keep the scandal from getting out."

Lottie felt the warmth of the woman's breath on her cheek, as she hissed into her ear.

What did Lady Anne know about love and respect? What did she know about Amelia and the reasons she left the care of her aunt? What scandal?

Lottie doubted Lady Anne's motives were anything but selfish, especially when the woman had the audacity to voice her request. Surely she was fishing to see if Lottie knew any more than she.

"To keep that particular secret safe, and to cover my prolonged stay at Ringwood to help Miss Amelia with the running of the manor, I ask for a small monthly stipend from the Gilroy estate."

Lottie's impatience with the woman almost overrode her respect for the house they stood in, and she very nearly raised her voice. However, Holmes happened by at that precise moment and diffused the situation.

"Lady Anne, as you have made quite clear on many occasions, Lottie is a maid. As such, she does not have any authority by which to make such an agreement." His voice, though quiet, filled the space in which the trio stood.

Lady Anne's mouth opened and closed, opened and closed, and Lottie was reminded of the carp in the river that ran through the estate.

"May I suggest you make an appointment with Mr. Forbes at his office? I would be happy to drive you there in the carriage."

Naturally, this was not agreeable to the lady, and she turned with such force that Lottie's cap was nearly blown from her head.

***

Lady Anne's cryptic words about Amelia's scandal stayed with Lottie for the rest of the day and into the night.

The night of the funeral, she felt so guilty about reading three of the fifteen letters that were sent from a loving niece to her aunt seeking forgiveness, that she crept back to the study and replaced the stack of envelopes behind the secret panel. If Lady Anne had not discovered the will before Lottie went to retrieve it at her mistress' bidding, she would not find the letters there.

She had no idea of the reason for Amelia's flight, apart from the fact that she believed herself to be desperately in love with a man some years older than her, who held her happiness in his hands.

Now, she wished she had learned more about Miss Amelia Colton. Despite Lottie's station in life as a housemaid, where she was comfortable and safe, she did have long-held ambitions that stretched beyond the servant's quarters.

A plan started to form in her mind, but it was several days before she felt brave enough to speak to Lady Anne.

"Milady, why do you require a stipend?"

Her directness took the woman by surprise, her eyebrows arching almost to her hairline.

"It is none of your business, you impudent girl. How dare you question a lady so?" Lady Anne's voice was shrill, but Lottie continued.

"I dare because you would not have stayed so long if you had your own comfortable accommodations to return to in Bath. I suggest you only came to Ringwood because you thought Lady Gilroy would remember you in her will," Lottie said, her voice steady.

She was emboldened by the unattractive creep of puce on the woman's neck and cheeks.

"I can offer you a proposition." She leaned in, her eyes locking with Lady Anne's. "Introduce me as Amelia into society. Act as my chaperone until I secure a husband."

Lady Anne's gaze flickered. She had her own agenda, of that Lottie was certain, and she wondered exactly what she would be willing to do in order to bring that to fruition.

As much as Lottie cared not a jot for this woman, it was clear that she would need Lady Anne in order to carry out her plan. The partnership offered mutual benefits, and the lady had already showed her hand in part.

"What will be required from me?" Any pretence at being affronted was gone, and the Lady was matter of fact.

Lottie's lips curved, but she curbed her pleasure at being able to turn someone to her will.

"Your connections in London society," she said. "Your influence. Your ability to shape my path. You will be my chaperone in public, and you will get the exposure you desire. Possibly even a husband of your own."

Lottie took a risk, making an assumption of what would motivate this greedy woman. But she was right, her logic sound. If Lady Anne helped her become established in society, if she married well, that would leave Anne alone. Naturally, she would want the same out of the deal, someone whose money she could spend as she wished.

A deal was struck—a pact forged in shadows, and the two partners struck a truce.

Holmes noticed the change in temperature in Lady Anne's way of addressing Lottie, once ice cold and derogatory, now cool and merely terse.

Lottie was honest with Holmes and Maggie from the start of this pact, and although they were surprised at her plan, they promised they would keep her counsel and support her.

***

Miss Amelia Colton, a name that clung to her like the scent of roses in a forgotten garden, stepped into her new existence. The transformation was both exhilarating and treacherous—a masquerade that would either elevate her or unravel her fragile web of deceit.

The silk gowns whispered against her skin, their opulence a stark contrast to the coarse fabric of her former life. Lottie—the maid—had vanished, leaving behind the mundane tasks and hidden corridors. Now, she was Amelia—the heiress.

But doubts gnawed at her. Could she maintain the charade? The letters—their ink still fresh in her memory—were helping her get to know Amelia. Lottie hid them away from Lady Anne's prying eyes but retrieved them back from the hidden panel in the desk, stealing moments to read a little at a time. The truth was both a burden and a lifeline.

Lady Anne, the cold enabler of this charade, clearly enjoyed her role as governess. She drilled Lottie—now Amelia—in the ways of the ton. Family history, societal norms, the art of dancing, walking, sitting, and fanning oneself—the lessons blurred into a dizzying whirl. When to laugh, when to smile, how to flutter her eyelashes—the rules were as intricate as the lace on her evening gloves.

Lottie arose early, retired late, and slept the sleep of the dead. Fatigue clung to her like cobwebs, but she pressed on. Never had she imagined her life taking this turn—the path from servant to heiress. But she had made the choice—to honour the real Amelia, to represent the Gilroy family with every breath she took.

As the sun dipped below the horizon, casting shadows across the grand manor, Lottie wondered if she could keep the illusion intact. The silk gowns rustled, and the secrets whispered. She squared her shoulders, determined to play her part. For Lady Eleanor, for herself, and for the enigmatic Amelia—the girl who had vanished, leaving behind a legacy of questions and unspoken truths. Bit by bit, even if the answers were not in her letters, Lottie would make it her mission to find the truth, as well as find herself a husband.

Chapter 5

Lottie, her heart aflutter like a caged bird, embarked on the journey to London, returning to the hometown she had fled from many years before. Lady Eleanor had travelled to the city several times when Lottie first went into her service, but the maid was too young to accompany her mistress on those occasions.

But her former home was not the focus of her thoughts. The Easter Ball—a glittering affair hosted by a distant cousin of Lady Anne's—loomed large in just a few days, its promise of intrigue and masked identities both thrilling and terrifying.

Holmes drove them in the Gilroy coach—a vessel of polished wood and gleaming brass, which had not been used much since Lady Eleanor kept to the manor. Both humans and horses rested at Midhurst, at the Spread Eagle coaching inn.

While Holmes cleaned, fed, and watered the horses before retiring to the public bar for the evening, Maggie, in her new role as ladies' maid, was to tend to both Lottie and Lady Anne. Lottie knew there was no love lost between Lady Anne and the Holmeses, they had taken an instant dislike to her disdainful manner. But they both loved Lottie, and she them, and they had decided they would support her in her escapade.

The inn, full of many secrets and much scandal over the centuries, provided a welcome distraction for the butterflies in Lottie's stomach. She sat in the window seat in her room, overlooking the main road, as she waited for Maggie to dress Lady Anne for dinner, reading a history of the inn and the town, with its royal and political connections.

When Maggie returned and was lacing up her corset, Lottie confessed her nerves. The silk gown clung to her like a second skin, and the weight of Lady Eleanor's legacy pressed upon her.

"What if I falter?" she whispered, her reflection in the mirror a stranger's face. "What if people see straight through the façade? What if I forget the steps to the cotillion or move the wrong way?"

"Sounds like something you'd make a dress out of. Now, listen, you're the best of any rich girl who'll grace that ball," Maggie turned Lottie to her, as she spoke fiercely. "And if it all goes awry, my girl, we'll retreat to Ringwood. Carry on as if nothing happened."

Maggie hugged her tight, her starched apron smelling faintly of freshly baked bread, a lingering reminder of the home they had left in Winchester.

Lottie nodded, her resolve bolstered. Tonight, taking their meal in the inn's dining room would be a good test of Lottie's nerves when meeting people who did not know the truth. If those on the outside treated her as they might any young lady, with pink cheeks, excited to be travelling with her chaperone to the brightly lit ballrooms of the capital, all would be well.

***

In the carriage, Lottie's stomach let out a growl, and Lady Anne gave her a dagger of a look, but softened her expression by handing the girl a piece of dried fruit that she carried in her reticule for just such situations.

"Forgive me, Lady Anne. It's been hours since luncheon, and my stomach thinks my throat's been cut," Lottie demurred.

"*Quelle horreur.*" Lady Anne shivered at the imagery created by Lottie's vivid description; the phrase one she had heard from Holmes after a busy day at work.

The girl bit back a smile as she chewed gratefully on the shrivelled apricot, willing her insides to behave. The closer the date drew to the Easter Ball, and the nearer the carriage drew to first London and now the Star and Garter Tavern and Hotel in Richmond, Lady Anne developed an amusing habit of dropping French phrases into the conversation.

Lottie knew this one meant how awful, and she had also learned some other tidbits. Never having met a real French person, she wondered how correct the Lady's pronunciation was, but she assured Lottie that the facial expression, the widening or narrowing of the eyes, the positioning of one's lips were key to authenticity.

They arrived, and footmen in powdered wigs and bright red jackets with golden braiding opened the carriage doors and handed both women safely to the ground and into the building. Even the entrance to the Star and Garter—which Lottie had mistakenly imagined to be akin to the coaching inn at Midhurst—was the grandest she had ever seen. The ceilings soared above them, and ahead the ballroom awaited—a cavern of chandeliers and beautiful people.

Lottie walked slightly behind Lady Anne, peering around her as they made their approach. They joined a short queue of guests, who were individually announced into the room; however, when it was their turn, Lottie did not think that anyone paid the slightest bit of attention.

The enormous ballroom was awash with sounds, delightful music from the harp and pianoforte played by musicians, male and female voices mingled in the air. As Lady Anne curtsied to a group of elderly ladies, who fell upon her like she was a long-lost sister, Lottie scanned the assembly, the largest number of fancily dressed people that she had ever seen in her life. And she was one of them.

Lottie brushed the pale-yellow silk self-consciously, feeling exposed without her cape and hat, surrendered to another servant upon their entrance. How she would ever get the correct items back at the end of the evening, she could not fathom. Her gown, the most beautiful she had ever worn, was almost bland next to the other ladies. The embroidery, the lace, the braiding was exquisite and quite beyond her own skills, even possibly those of Maggie, an experienced needlewoman.

As the women swallowed Lady Anne into their midst, she could see the ladies on the outer edge casting judgemental glances, their fans concealing sneers, their wine glasses hiding whispered judgements.

One younger beautiful woman, whose smile was a beacon of warmth, stepped forward and took Lottie's hand.

"You are most welcome, my dear. I am Freya."

Lady Anne glanced over her shoulder as if belatedly remembering the reason for their presence and twisted her neck like an owl as she recognised what was happening. Turning and curtsying at the same time, she made the introduction.

"Duchess Antcliffe, a pleasure. May I introduce Miss Amelia Colton, niece of the late Lady Eleanor Gilroy."

Freya nodded to Lady Anne, and her smile widened as Lottie dropped into the deepest curtsy she could manage and squeaked a reply.

"Your Grace."

The rest of the group, their faces etched with history, welcomed her gladly, and for a moment, Lottie believed in her own masquerade.

Freya stayed a few moments, listening to the conversation, paying particular attention to Lottie and Lady Anne before she moved on.

An hour later, after following Lady Anne around the room, listening to her talk about people, places, and events that she had no idea about, Lottie was sure she would faint from hunger. The Duchess rescued Lottie, looping her arm in hers.

"My Lady, if I might borrow your young charge," Freya said graciously to Lady Anne before leading Lottie directly to the dining room.

Lottie ate gratefully, remembering her manners, and spent an enjoyable interlude learning about Freya and her three daughters and, in turn, telling her new friend of the delights of living at the manor.

As they walked about the ballroom, where the dancers moved gracefully around the dance floor, Lottie was secretly thrilled that her saviour had singled her out. Freya's station in life created immediate deference, and the ladies and gentlemen bobbed and bowed as she passed, pausing whatever they were doing, be it gossiping, eating, or drinking.

Freya told Lottie about the other young ladies in the room and introduced her to several handsome and polite young men. Lottie smiled, curtsied, laughed, and remained quiet at the appropriate times, her nerves dancing along the edge of a precipice, as she tried to remember names and faces.

Lottie caught the eye of a tall man with wide shoulders and dark hair swept back from his forehead. He was a very late arrival and drew a lot of attention, especially from the young women out in society. She remembered seeing him at Lady Eleanor's funeral, and she stepped out of his line of sight to hide from his unwanted scrutiny.

Freya was amused to see Lottie's reaction but also saw how Lord Audley-Sinclair was headed, most determined, across the room toward them, only to be waylaid by every unattached girl.

"The most eligible bachelor in the country, I feel, Lottie," Freya explained, and Lottie knew exactly who she was referring to. "He will never get married, has the most frightful reputation, and he only dances with the most beautiful women. Not exactly husband material."

The man bore down on Freya and Lottie, towering over them with a glower. This softened as he greeted Freya.

"Your Grace, as beautiful as ever." He bowed to kiss the back of her hand, and Freya smiled. "Is your husband here to keep you safe from all your thwarted suitors, milady?"

"My Lord, yes, he is about, but I am quite capable of keeping myself secure." Freya smiled. "Let me introduce my new friend, this is her first time at an Easter Ball, my Lord."

Freya moved to bring Lottie forward, but all she wanted to do was run and hide. The man looked like he wanted to devour her, and she was unsure why her body was shaking slightly in response.

"Miss Colton and I are previously acquainted, your Grace," he informed Freya, turning to face Lottie. "Would you do me the honour of dancing with me?"

He bowed. Lottie glanced at Freya, who nudged her, and Lottie curtsied, allowing him to lead her to the dance floor where a quadrille was just about to start.

As the couples took formation, bowing and curtsying as was custom, Lottie bit her lip and danced in silence with the man. She focused on remembering the steps, but when he took her hand, the warmth of his skin radiated through her. Despite her uncertainty, she took pleasure in being led by someone so self-assured. Lady Anne tried to lead her when they practiced, and when she rehearsed with Maggie or Holmes, they usually ended in fits of laughter.

Not a word was spoken, and the man did not meet her eye once, just looked right through her. By the end of the dance, Lottie was confused and a little embarrassed, both from the lack of conversation but also from the looks she was at the receiving end of as they moved around the dance floor.

She was desperate to get away, to retreat to the safety of Lady Anne's group of older women, surely perfectly safe from this man. However, once the dance had ended, she turned to curtsy to him, but his eyes burned her, his gaze bold, taking her in from head to toe.

"Thank you, my Lord," Lottie whispered and turned to go, but he held her hand tightly.

He held her gaze, and Lottie was horrified as the musicians started up a waltz, and the man pulled her closer. All the air left her lungs as if sucked in by the collective gasp of every unattached girl in the room.

The waltz, only newly accepted into society by the Almack, was still risqué, but the man did not seem to care. His eyes locked with Lottie's, as they moved as one around the floor. She was amazed her feet knew what to do, but following his lead was as easy as she sensed it was dangerous.

The waltz ended, and Lottie caught her breath, her cheeks warm from the exertion and the close contact to this man. There seemed to be a huge silence in the room, as everyone watched expectantly. It was improper for a young lady to engage in more than two consecutive dances with an eligible man, and almost indecent at how Lottie felt after spending several minutes in this man's strong arms.

Lottie waited for the Lord to release his hold, to bow and thank her for her company. It took what felt like an eternity before he let go, and Lottie took a step to balance herself. He nodded curtly, turned his back on her, and left her standing on the dance floor alone.

The fans came out, and Lottie heard the rustle of whispers, like the dry autumn leaves on a tree, blown by a breeze. She knew she was the subject of their gossip, and she looked around, panic welling in her stomach.

Lady Anne and Freya headed straight for her, from different sides of the room, and Freya reached her first. She brought the dizzy, confused Lottie to a private salon for refreshments.

"My dear, you look positively overcome," Freya cooed, as she guided Lottie to a chaise longue.

Lottie could only watch as Freya waved her hand to a nearby servant, waiting patiently with his hands behind his back, to bring refreshments. The young man filled two glasses with red liquid, placed both on a silver platter, and brought them over. With a bow, he offered the platter to Lottie, who took a glass and drank it straight down. The drink was sweet, fruity, and rather refreshing, and she was suddenly very thirsty.

"It's delicious," she told the young man, as she replaced the empty glass and took the second, drinking that a little slower, but not much. "Thank you."

"Drink it slowly, for it is quite strong." Freya sat beside her, and gently pushed Lottie's hand down, bringing the glass to her lap.

With a very slight incline of her head, Freya dismissed the servant, who returned to his former position, waiting for the next guest who needed his service.

There were several other ladies in the salon, seated across the room, and Lottie watched them with open interest as they drank the red liquid and laughed at some secret fun.

"The Earl of Bevanbrook gave every appearance of being very taken with you, Amelia. Almost unheard of for him to dance even one full dance with a young lady, never mind two. He is previously acquainted with you, perhaps that familiarity makes him bold in his attention." Freya's voice was gentle, and it took Lottie a moment to realise she was talking to her.

And then another moment to register a name she did not recognise. She thought back to the who's who lessons with Lady Anne, but she did not believe she knew of an Earl of Bevanbrook.

Confusion must have shown on her face because Freya smiled gently and removed the glass from Lottie's hand.

"I understand you have been out of society for a while, as well as out of the country, my dear. Perhaps you knew him previously as Lord Audley-Sinclair. He only became Earl two years since, after the death of his older brother, who inherited the Earldom from his father."

Lottie nodded. That was the name she recognised. The Lord who had glared at her so harshly when she was introduced to him as Miss Amelia Colton at the funeral, as if he knew something that she did not.

She was minded to keep her distance from the gentleman, as she did not like how he made her feel, just as she was starting to feel like she could pull off this masquerade. Especially as he did have a reputation and was not husband material. She would not give the man, Earl or Lord, any more thought.

Chapter 6

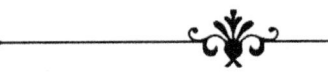

Yesterday evening's Easter Ball might have been yet another boring affair had it not been for the discovery of a new young lady out in society with whom he was not yet familiar. The delightful Duchess Antcliffe had been at her side and she would no doubt be more than willing to afford him an introduction.

When Nathaniel had laid eyes on her, her wide-eyed expression, the pinkness of her cheeks, her shining eyes drew him across the room. By the time he arrived, he was frustrated by the distractions and saw the girl recoil as he stood over them. Shame if she was shy and retiring; she was surely as attractive as any other girl in the room. He liked them with spirit, even if it was only to dance with.

After he had flattered the Duchess sufficiently, and she began to make the introduction, the memory of the last time he had met this girl hit him hard in the chest, catching his breath. Last time, her face had been covered with the veil, her grief palpable. But now, she stood before him, radiant in her yellow silk, and his initial attraction was replaced with the determination to get her to reveal her truth.

Their first dance the previous evening had been a boring quadrille, and yet her lightness of step, the smile on her lips that he did not believe she was aware of, taunted him, stalling his mission. He wanted to interrogate her, intimidate her into confession, but no words came forth. Hence, he had pressed his lips together until he was sure he could drive the conversation forward.

He had every intention of letting her go at the end of the dance, for there would surely be plenty of opportunity throughout this season, if she was out, to get what he wanted from her. The strains of the intoxicating waltz started up, and the opportunity to hold her close, to feel her against him was quite more than he expected.

So, he did not release her, instead leading her through uncharted territory. She intrigued him beyond words, and he hungered for more, a taste of her hidden truths. Her body was lithe under his hands, her waist neatly curved, her neck pale and elegant as she tilted it becomingly away from him as they danced.

But Nathaniel was a man of contradictions, and he was certainly contradicted now. He loved women—their laughter, their curves, their whispered promises. Especially the older, married kind. Molly, the red-haired beauty from Belgravia, had been his willing accomplice in many a stolen moment.

Yet Amelia—this enigmatic version of her—drew him like a moth to a flame. She held secrets he wanted to know, and yet he knew the truth, or at least his version of it.

His body flamed to life, and his thoughts started down a forbidden path that ought not be trodden in public, and as regret warred with lust, he released Amelia from his hold so suddenly that she took a step back. At once, he wanted to pull her to his body, but instead, he nodded and stalked away.

Nathaniel knew his dismissal of her set societal tongues wagging, and he felt the whispers carry him out of the ballroom, through the huge doors, and down the steps like a river flowing to the sea. His slight to Miss Amelia Colton would not go unnoticed and would not reflect well upon her. A gentleman would not leave a young lady on the dance floor but would accompany her back to her party.

In the night air, he took a deep breath to clear Amelia from his mind. She did not deserve to have space there, not when he knew she was definitely not who she claimed to be. Anger built in him as he waited for his carriage, but he could not express it for fear of revealing his own secrets. They were locked away in the vaults of his heart, and he could not, absolutely would not risk the truth being revealed.

His rakish exploits, the dalliances that fuelled London's gossip mills, were a mere façade. He would never share the truth with anyone, not even the wonderful Molly.

At the thought of the redhead's creamy curves, the desire to lose himself in the secret valleys of Molly's body was paramount, and he instructed the driver to take him to his paramour's house. Tomorrow there would be time enough to think about Miss Amelia Colton, whomever she may be. Tonight, he would forget and sink into the arms of a woman who had no need to pretend to be anything else.

***

Another ball awaited the next day, one to which Nathaniel had originally declined the invitation. His sources whispered of a bevy of young ladies, fresh from the cocoons of their mothers' bosoms, pushed from the familial nest into the societal hunting grounds in search of a suitable husband.

Among them, he hoped to find Amelia, and he relished the chance to delve deeper into her mystery, to see the blush on her cheeks, the fire in her eyes as he asked her to dance again. The girl had disturbed his slumber, keeping his mind dancing long after he had left her standing on the dance floor.

Nathaniel arrived slightly earlier than usual, and there she was—a vision in burnt copper silk, Miss Amelia Colton. Her hair, piled high in a concoction of curls and ribbons, defied the rigid norms. Pink cheeks, untouched by rouge, lent her a natural beauty that outshone any other young debutante in the room. His gaze lingered, assessing, amused at her shyness, as she moved around the room with Lady Anne.

This evening, he intended to play with her, tease her, leave her guessing as to his true intentions. It was expected—the dance of courtship, the push against accepted boundaries.

She would be unable to withstand his advances, flattered by his attention, confused by the feelings he awoke in her. She was young, that was very obvious, and inexperienced in the ways of sophisticated society. Nathaniel watched her look to Lady Anne and, when joined by the Duchess Antcliffe, to her new friend for guidance.

Amelia reminded him of another, when first introduced to society nearly a decade since, shy, nervous, but inquisitive. That was the first time he had ever felt the need to protect anyone but himself, inspiring the same feeling that he had first encountered on the battlefields in France. That was the first time he had acted like a true gentleman, cherishing the girl as a big brother would his little sister.

He felt no such need now, only an urge to uncover and expose the true identity of the chit masquerading as Amelia.

Nathaniel headed for the group surrounding Amelia, and the unattached females all dropped their fans, fluttered their eyelids, and eyed him covertly, as they curtsied. Amelia, the only one he had eyes for, averted her gaze, her jaw tense, and merely bobbed.

Her silent rebellion to tradition irked him but also reminded him of the determination of the real Amelia.

"Miss Colton," Nathaniel's words were clipped as he bowed and held out his hand.

As he straightened, he noted the lift of Amelia's chin, and he wondered for a moment if she dared defy his invitation to dance. She would be within her rights, given his insulting behaviour the previous evening, but it would be a death knell to her chances of being invited to the upper echelons of social gatherings. It was not just his eyes on her, but the entire room.

Amelia met his gaze squarely, and just as she was about to make her response, Lady Anne nudged her in the ribs with her fan, and Nathaniel knew he had won in their war of wills. Lady Anne, as chaperone, was obviously keen for Amelia to make the best match, even if her ward was nowhere as enthusiastic about the opportunity.

Nathaniel led her through the first dance, enjoying the charged atmosphere in the ballroom. The music provided a backdrop to their silent conversation, and yet he heard her unspoken words loud and clear. She did not like him, she was not enjoying herself, and she could not wait to get away from him.

So different from every single female in the room, and probably a number of those who were married and in the company of their husbands. They would die for the chance to be held by Lord Audley-Sinclair, possibly a once-in-a-lifetime fantasy that would carry them through their staid marriages, the thrill of contact with the man of their dreams.

Amelia moved defiantly at his side as they danced, her countenance pleasant, but her eyes did not meet his, her smile, when required, held no warmth, and in his hold, she put as much space between them as she could.

The music ended while they were out of hold, and Amelia met his eyes, curtsied, and started to turn back to her party.

"Amelia." Nathaniel took a step toward her and took her wrist, pulling her toward him.

Her voice was cold and quiet, as she turned to face him.

"I thank you for your patronage, this evening and last. I shall save you the embarrassment of dancing another with me, sir."

The musicians readied their instruments, and Amelia took the cue, tugging her hand free of his, and bobbed once more, clearly desperate to be out of his presence. Nathaniel wondered momentarily at her choice of words and recognised the embarrassment would be completely his if she left the dance floor alone.

"Miss Colton, forgive my ungentlemanly behaviour." He bowed deeply, with a flourish. "It would make me happy to dance another with you."

He straightened, expecting her to clutch her hand to her chest, ready to swoon, but instead, the start of a smile tickled the corners of her mouth, and her eyes sparkled with amusement.

The music started, and the dancers took their positions. Nathaniel's instinct was to take her in his arms like a possession, to hold her tightly. The ballroom was their battleground, however, and he was ready for the war.

Women, their fans like shields, cast dagger-sharp looks at this newcomer. Men watched jealously, wanting to be him—the man who held Amelia's gaze. Yet, good manners required the young lady's acquiescence, especially as her intent was to get away.

"If it makes the *gentleman* happy," Amelia murmured, lowering her head slightly, before taking his proffered hand.

He noticed the inflection of the word gentleman and decided, under such scrutiny, he ought to behave himself or at least appear to be on his best behaviour. And another dance in silence was not good form.

"How are you enjoying your introduction to society, Miss Colton? Is it much different from society in Hampshire?"

Conversation was expected, but the audience did not need to know how loaded his question of the young lady was.

"I have made several pleasant acquaintances, my Lord." Her tone made it clear that she did not include him on that list. "As for society in Hampshire, I have little experience of such, for my time was fully dedicated to the care and comfort of my Lady Eleanor."

"Yes, your dear aunt. My condolences once more." Nathaniel recognised a carefully crafted answer when he heard one, a frequently used tool in his own defensive arsenal. "You may remember my late mother and Lady Eleanor were dear friends."

He looked down at Amelia's face as he spoke to watch for her reaction. As a gentleman, a member of the ton, he should rise above his peevish behaviour. In his chosen profession, hidden from view, covert by its very nature, lies were par for the course, but he could not stand for it in his everyday life.

Surely this young woman would prefer not to be a part of his life, but until he got to her truth, he would make it his purpose to unmask her.

"I am sincerely sorry for your own loss, Lord Audley-Sinclair. Lady Eleanor spoke of your mother with great warmth."

At last, her tone of voice and the shine in her eyes matched her words, meant with kindness and a fleeting sense of understanding. But he could not let her win him over with her pretty face and captivating eyes.

They danced in silence while Nathaniel pondered how to get her to reveal herself, and before he knew it, the music ended, and he bowed as she curtsied to him. Dare he dance with her for a third, without bringing too much attention to both himself and his quarry?

"You are forgiven, my Lord," Amelia murmured, and for a moment, Nathaniel did not understand her reference.

The girl was clear in her meaning as she turned slightly toward her party, raising her hand. He took her signal and her hand and escorted her back to Lady Anne and the others.

She was intelligent, that much was clear, but while he did not push his attention for further dances, he kept close to her side as Lady Anne, the Duchess Antcliffe, and other ladies ebbed and flowed in conversation. Amelia garnered attention from both men and women, and it did not take long as Nathaniel left to gather refreshments for the ladies for other young men to head for her shining light.

As much as her chaperone and the Duchess provided a barrier for the young woman, Nathaniel brooded and bristled each time another young buck dared to approach for a formal introduction.

Manners forgotten, Nathaniel stood at the shoulder of the latest would-be suitor, his presence an immediate deterrent.

"Madam, I beg your company for the next dance," Nathaniel said and reclaimed Amelia's hand.

The dance floor was theirs, and they twisted and turned, secrets swirling like confetti between them.

"Where have you been, Miss Colton?" Nathaniel pulled her tightly against him, their contact closer than the waltz required, an awkward intimacy wrapping itself around them. "Hiding in Hampshire all the while?"

She stared deep into his eyes, probing, and he began to feel uncomfortable, unsettled. This was how she was supposed to be feeling, out of place, out of her depth, not him. Could she read his intentions, were they so clear on his face, in his actions?

"Hiding, my Lord, like a child waiting to be discovered?"

The discomfort stirred his stomach, akin to the nervous anticipation, the momentary fear he felt right before he led his men into battle.

There was no conceivable possibility where this young pretender could know his deepest secrets, no matter how good her pretence at being another.

Amelia, the girl with the question in her eyes, would be his challenge—a puzzle he intended to solve, even if it meant unravelling his own defences.

Chapter 7

Lord Audley-Sinclair waltzed into Lottie's life like a hurricane. His eyes held secrets—dark and beguiling, and she felt herself under scrutiny, and not just from his Lordship. She could not forget how he claimed her attention in two candlelit ballrooms just days before, setting tongues wagging, creating a reputation she neither wanted nor deserved.

Lady Anne had been full of her own self-importance as they returned home to Ringwood, satisfied that she had successfully not only introduced Lottie into society as Amelia but firmly embedded her in the marriage market.

"So many eligible young men vying for your attention, my girl, and yet your time monopolised by a Lord, no less. My connections in society are deeply rooted, and I have not been forgotten in my long absence."

"Your introductions were invaluable, my Lady," Lottie muttered and looked out of the window of the coach as the scenery became more familiar.

They would soon be at the manor.

"There cannot be any doubt that I have fulfilled the terms of our agreement. I will expect payment on the morrow, child, and I must return to my own home in Bath. I have a long-standing prior engagement that I must attend."

Lottie nodded politely and agreed that Holmes would effect payment in the morning and see to it that Lady Anne would be connected with the stagecoach in Winchester to return to Bath.

That evening, Lottie retired to her room in the attic, glad to be in her own company, in her own bed. She had offered to attend to

Lady Anne's needs, along with Maggie, as they were now able to return to their usual roles, but Maggie told her there was plenty of time for that once their guest had gone.

Lottie longed to retrieve Amelia's letters from their hiding place where she had reluctantly left them days before they departed for London. Knowing Lady Anne's predilection for snooping, Lottie had not felt safe bringing the letters with her. She had yet to read more than half a dozen, which gave her some understanding of Amelia but left many gaps she longed to fill with the truth.

She would wait a little longer, until their guest had departed, to be sure she would be the only keeper of Amelia's secrets. Instead, her thoughts turned to Lord Audley-Sinclair and the mixture of feelings he caused in her. The man was as ill-mannered as he was handsome, as arrogant as he had been attentive. Lady Anne and her new friend Freya had expected her to be flattered by the dedication of the Lord's attention, ensuring that she knew how out of character it was.

The man liked to taunt her, and some of his questions, however innocent, left her in no doubt he held her in judgement. She was unsure if he suspected that she was not who she pretended to be or if he just did not like her. Why waste so much effort and time on her if it was the latter? However, she should prefer his disdain over discovery.

The next day, Lottie watched Lady Anne depart with a mixture of relief for a return to normality in the manor and some uncertainty about how to move forward without the Lady's patronage.

Lottie spent the next few days helping Maggie take in and customise some dresses they found in the attic, which Lottie assumed were Amelia's. Fascinated by this young woman, she cherished the time each night she could read Amelia's next letter to her aunt.

Amelia, it seemed, had shockingly eloped with an older man with whom she had fallen in love. The gentleman had been injured during the war and returned to the barrack town of Winchester, where Amelia had visited with the veteran soldiers on a regular basis as a young woman.

Lottie, although truly shocked, thought her namesake brave, and even more so when she read in greater detail the truth of the matter in the next letter. Amelia identified that she found herself unexpectedly with child and worried the father of her unborn child would deny her once she told him. The despair in the words on the page touched Lottie, and she understood from her own experience how it felt to be alone as a child.

Grateful that Lady Eleanor, for whatever reason, had not read the letters, Lottie thought about the shame that would have been brought upon the family if the truth had been revealed. Society would judge freely and with vigorous ferocity.

Just as Lottie was reading the joy in Amelia's next letter, dated some months later, the doorbell rang, and Lottie assumed it was a delivery. Returning her attention to the neat handwriting, Amelia's letter spoke of her happiness for her and her unborn baby. Amelia had been reunited with the man she admired, respected, and for whom she felt great affection. She was grateful that her baby would have a father figure who would take care of them, no matter what.

Jolted out of her reverie, Lottie registered a man's voice in discussion with the northern chime of Maggie's. The voices grew louder, approaching the library at the back of the house, where Lottie was ensconced on the window seat. Desperate to know the man's identity, she read his name, just as Maggie opened the library door and announced the visitor.

Lord Nathaniel Audley-Sinclair. One and the same.

Lottie had time to fold the letter and tuck it under the cushion of the window seat before she stood to greet her visitor.

"My Lord, this is an unexpected honour," Lottie said deferentially as she curtsied. "Lady Anne has returned to her home for a short while. You find me unattended."

By rights, for propriety's sake, she should not receive her visitor without a chaperone, and Maggie lingered awaiting instruction.

"Miss Colton, I apologise for arriving unannounced. I had business in Winchester and desired to pay my respects to Lady Anne and yourself."

He bowed deeply, and Lottie watched his dark curls fall forward. An urge to brush a wayward strand of hair tickled her fingertips, and she clenched her fists tightly at her sides. Such a gesture would be most unwelcome to this gentleman, she was certain. The fact he stood in her home was disconcerting but also thrilling.

To see him in a different setting, out of context, combined with the way his gaze slid toward Maggie waiting patiently and his less than perfect coiffeur gave him an air of vulnerability.

Whether he knew it or not, was a different matter.

Lottie nodded to Maggie, who stepped forward to take his hat, coat, and riding crop.

"Will you require refreshments, ma'am?" Maggie asked, pausing by the door.

"Yes, please," Lottie answered, without consulting her guest, but gestured with her hand and a gentle smile that he could make himself comfortable on the chaise by the fire.

But he did not take her offer. Instead, he paced the length of the room, picking up books, giving her long looks, and then shifting his attention elsewhere. There were seemingly interminable moments of silence in the few minutes before Maggie brought tea.

"How does my Lord prefer his tea?" Lottie bent her head as she arranged Lady Eleanor's best bone china cups just so.

Thoughtfully, Maggie placed a saucer of finely sliced lemon, along with the jug of milk and sugar bowl, and Lottie sent silent thanks her way. Freya had told Lottie, who had told Maggie, that lemon in black tea was currently *de rigeur* among high society, especially amongst those who frequented the Continent. She firmly expected Lord Audley-Sinclair to opt for it.

"Strong, black, one sugar."

Lottie obliged and brought his tea to him as he stood by the window. Their hands touched for a brief moment as he took the cup, and her skin prickled with awareness. She was also overtly aware of the letter under the window seat cushion behind him. She hoped that he would not think to take repose on the very seat under which Amelia's letter was hidden.

"I hope you are well, Miss Colton," he asked, before taking a mouthful of the hot liquid.

A momentary look of satisfaction lifted his eyebrows, and a tiny nod indicated he approved of his beverage. Lottie took her seat at the table and lifted her own china cup and saucer.

"I am, milord. I trust you, too, are in good health?"

He inclined his head but was not so inclined to answer, it appeared, and Lottie wondered why he had come all this way out of town to visit with her when he barely made her acquaintance. What did he hope to get out of their encounter?

The way he looked at her intrigued her; his expression sometimes quizzical with wide eyes, at other times, suspicious with a narrowed gaze. What did he know about her; what did he suspect? Lottie wondered how she could come to know it too.

Lottie was playing at being Amelia Colton, and she was quickly learning that life in society was a series of moves in order to win the game, to gain a husband as a prize. While Lottie had no designs on nor desire for this arrogant aristocrat, she was smart enough to know she would have to dance with him in more ways than one to get to know him better.

"I confess, Lord Audley-Sinclair, I am beyond flattered that you have paid a visit to Ringwood Manor," she demurred, fluttering her eyelashes as she had seen other young ladies do at a gentleman they were enamoured of.

"Don't be," came his calm retort, and Lottie's pride prickled at the insult, no matter how mildly delivered.

To her embarrassment, tears filled her eyes and she blinked them away, just as he looked at her. She hoped he did not think she was in any way trying to ingratiate herself with him still. He had quashed that sentiment.

Lord Audley-Sinclair tilted his head slightly as he took another sip of his tea, and Lottie saw a spark light in his eyes.

"You intrigue me, Miss Colton."

Now she had an opponent in this game, and he clearly thought he had the upper hand. But Lottie was more than he thought her to be, some silly girl looking for a husband. She had discovered at the very moment of his arrival at the manor of his intimate connection with Amelia, which meant he knew that she, Lottie, was not the real Miss Colton. And this is where she might just have the upper hand, and the next move was hers to make. She was feeling brave, safe in her secret knowledge.

"What line of business are you in, now you are retired from the Army, my Lord?"

"I anticipate we have more in common than you might think, *Amelia*, as we go about our daily business."

He moved toward the table, abruptly laid down his cup, spilling its remains into the saucer, the clatter making Lottie jump. His visit was clearly ended as he bowed and turned to leave.

Lottie followed him out to the hallway, and he waited for someone to bring his belongings. Maggie was clearly unaware of the requirement, so Lottie, stepping back into her former role, calmly collected his coat, hat, and crop and handed them to him.

Surprise wrote itself clearly on his countenance, and he bowed his farewell.

A frown drew his eyebrows together, deepening as he caught sight of something above Lottie's head. She turned to follow his gaze, realising she stood under Amelia's portrait. Whereas

Forbes, the solicitor, had seen a passing likeness, the shake of Lord Audley-Sinclair's head indicated a different reaction.

Maggie hurried into the hallway and looked momentarily stricken at the fully clothed Lord about to take his leave. She curtsied deeply as she opened the door, and once it was closed, Lottie and Maggie exchanged worried looks. Before either could speak, the doorbell rang once more, and Lottie felt her stomach turn in nervous anticipation. Was he back?

Maggie opened the door to the postman, who delivered an invitation from Duchess Antcliffe, Freya, inviting Lottie to join her in Bath at their country home. They were hosting a ball and Freya would be delighted if Lottie would join her family a few days before, along with Lady Anne, if the Lady so wished.

Lottie was thrilled to be invited, as she thought very well of Freya and looked forward to getting to know her better. She wondered if Lord Audley-Sinclair might be present, which drove her directly to the library to finish the letter she had stuffed down the back of the window seat cushion.

She needed to learn everything she could about this man in order to arm her for their next encounter. He was a professional soldier, used to battle. Lottie was merely a maid playing pretend as a lady of substance, yet, she had more to gain than she had to lose.

What did the Lord mean to Amelia, and more importantly, what did Amelia, and now Lottie, mean to him?

Chapter 8

Life with the Antcliffes was a revelation, Lottie found. The atmosphere in their sprawling country manor, at least four times the size of Ringwood Manor, was light and airy, and Freya's three daughters were happy and free. So different from how Lottie remembered her own childhood.

When she first arrived—was it only the day before?—Lottie had felt shy and out of her depth. With no Lady Anne behind whom to hide, she felt nervous about remembering how to behave and how to address the Duke and Duchess, and all the little nuances of speech, dress, and action. But she soon found that very little pretence was required or expected, apart from the tiny detail of remembering her new name.

Lottie curtsied deeper than she had ever done so in her life upon being introduced to Duke Christopher Antcliffe.

"I am delighted to meet you, Miss Colton. Freya has spoken of you nonstop since returning from London and forced me at gunpoint to hold a ball especially so she could introduce you to Bath society."

Lottie swallowed hard, and Freya caught her wide-eyed look and laughingly linked her arm.

"Do not believe a word out of His Grace's mouth, my dear, such shocking untruths as you will ever hear."

Her husband laughed aloud, and Lottie smiled at the deep, booming laugh that filled the salon room, putting her at ease instantly.

"I confess it." His Grace threw his hands up and was jumped upon by his youngest daughter. "Though you are a most welcome guest to Freshford, Miss Colton, if you will listen to my wife's nonstop chatter about the ball two days hence, for my own ears are surely soon to fall off."

"Papa has no ears!" The youngest girl announced loudly and clapped her small hands over her father's generous ears.

The three girls ran from the salon, screaming with mock fear and genuine laughter as their father chased after them, and Freya led Lottie through the French doors into the garden.

"You have a delightful family, your Grace," Lottie told her friend.

"We'll have no airs and graces between us, Amelia, for we are friends, are we not? I feel as if we have known each other for an age. I insist you will call me Freya, for that is my name."

There was no nuance to Freya's words, but Lottie stayed wary of any references, however loose or vague, to the real Amelia's past and any possible associations. First, Lord Audley-Sinclair had intimated of a connection between them, currently unqualified, and now this from Freya.

The three little girls had peppered their mother's new friend with a barrage of questions upon her arrival and many times since, and although polite with ingrained breeding, they had no filter. They thought nothing of asking about Lottie's own parents, her siblings, and her upbringing because that was the sphere of their experience. Lottie managed to deflect, infer, and confuse the children, but talking about such with an adult required far more wit and consideration.

"Lady Anne is due to arrive later this afternoon, I understand," Freya said, as they strolled along the edge of the large ornamental pond.

"You are very kind to include my Lady in your invitation. I know she is eternally grateful." Lottie was able to answer truthfully.

"No doubt," Freya smiled. "Lady Anne has long been on the fringes of Bath society, and I hate to think of her missing out still, even after all these years."

Lottie, who knew nothing of Lady Anne before her arrival at Ringwood Manor, took immediate interest. Lady Anne herself, throughout Lottie's lessons, had stressed how important it was to take an active interest in societal gossip, but never to initiate or be seen to enjoy such an activity. However, it was essential and polite to engage in pleasant conversation with one's hostess. But to enquire after the obvious would be too direct.

"Missing out?"

Freya continued conversationally.

"Lady Anne's late husband, Lord Boyatt Gilroy, was a most genial man, took great care of his appearance, and loved to dance, attending every ball, party, and gathering. Lady Anne, naturally, accompanied her husband, for appearance's sake. After his—" Freya lowered her voice. "—fall from grace, he and his wife were not much in company, and then his subsequent death further curtailed her presence in society, for the past decade at least."

"That would explain the way her friends in London seemed to welcome her like they'd been apart for an age."

Lottie wondered how Lord Audley-Sinclair's rumoured affairs with married women allowed him to continue to enjoy social gatherings when another man, such as Lord Boyatt Gilroy, was shunned.

"And the very same *friends* of Lady Anne tittle-tattled incessantly behind her back in London too, Lottie. Choose your friends wisely, my dear, as there are those who will take great joy in the misfortune of others."

Further conversation was delayed with the arrival of the three young girls pulling their father in his habitual hunting attire, followed by the gamekeeper and several groundsmen.

"My dear, your daughters wish to dance, but I've informed them I have two left feet and am now too deaf from their pleas to hear any music at all. I implore you and Miss Colton to entertain them so that I can retreat in peace to shoot something."

There was no ire or annoyance in the Duke's tone, and Lottie admired his dedication to his family's happiness.

"Indeed, your Grace." Freya inclined her head, and Lottie and the girls curtsied as the hunting party headed off.

The two women and the girls made their way to the ballroom, where the household staff were decorating ahead of the ball, and the rest of the afternoon passed so pleasantly, Lottie was surprised at the announcement of Lady Anne's arrival.

***

"Sit up straight, girl," Lady Anne hissed the next evening as the maid cleared the table following the main course.

A sharp elbow, which Lottie was sure her chaperone sharpened on a regular basis, to her ribs also put pay to any kind comment to the staff waiting at the table. Another black mark to blot Lottie's copybook, she was sure.

During their relatively short time apart, a matter of only a fortnight, Lottie wondered what had become of Lady Anne to put her in such a particularly picky mood. Nothing Lottie had done since they were reunited had passed muster, from the way she styled her hair—at Freya's suggestion—to the way she frolicked with the Duke and Duchess' daughters, to her deportment.

"Dearest Amelia, if you have any room left in that tiny figure of yours—" Sir James Holden, their host for the evening, reached out from the head of the table to her right and touched her hand. "—my chef has created the most extravagant Queen of Puddings for your delight."

Lottie smiled because she liked the older gentleman, closer in age to Lady Anne than to herself. His kindly attention fluctuated between flattery, which fell a little short of the mark, and fatherly patronage, which Lottie felt suited him well. However, this was another thing that peeved Lady Anne this evening.

"Sir James, you are too kind. Amelia's developed quite an appetite in my absence, I think she has enjoyed sufficient of your generous hospitality for one evening," Lady Anne commented before Lottie could respond.

The older woman had eaten like a bird at both the Freshford and Holden tables, despite gorging herself willingly at every meal at Ringwood Manor.

"Then I insist, my Lady, that you have double helpings of this delicious fare," Sir James laughed and raised his glass in toast.

Lottie fixed a smile to her face as she bore it as well as she could through the rest of the evening. She had been firmly put in her place by her chaperone, who smiled and giggled like a young woman at their host's humorous conversation.

At the end of the evening, Lottie gave her warm thanks to Sir James, who bowed as he held her hand a little longer than she expected.

"Until tomorrow evening, my dear. I hope to secure the first dance with you in the Freshford ballroom."

Lady Anne's lips pulled together tighter than a drawstring purse at the prolonged contact.

"That's if she can fit into her new dress, Sir James." Lady Anne gave a sneering laugh, and her comment landed ill with their host.

"I am sure Miss Colton will look handsome in the plainest of outfits, my Lady."

Lottie hid her grin, as Lady Anne hurried her out to the waiting Freshford carriage.

"Your time with the Duchess has given you ideas above your station, *Charlotte*." Lady Anne lasted but a minute before she set forth. "You are my ward, girl. You should remember your station, as such. I allowed you to come along, but it was I who was invited by Sir James to dine with him. How dare you monopolise so much of his time."

Lottie sat back, a flash of anger warming her cheeks in the darkness of the carriage. She had enjoyed the freedom of being welcomed into the Duke and Duchess' home as a friend, as Amelia, and taken exactly as she was. Now Lady Anne was back and determined to put Lottie back in her place. However, Lottie had other ideas.

"My lady, I am puzzled by your ire. Is not our ultimate contract to secure a good marriage?" Lottie leaned forward as the carriage passed a streetlamp and was able to meet her chaperone's gaze. "Secure a good marriage for me?"

There was no response to Lottie's mildly posed question, and as the carriage navigated the streets of Bath, a gentle snore emanated from the older woman sitting opposite. Lady Anne had imbibed much of the sweet wine that accompanied their meal, which, along with a double helping of the delicious-looking dessert, had rendered her somnolent.

Lottie gazed out of the window as the carriage paused at a busy intersection at the edge of what seemed to be a park. There were two figures, one dressed to the nines and another less well, standing under a streetlamp a little way along a path that divided the lawned area, and Lottie had to look again as she thought she recognised one of the men.

As the carriage driver took advantage of a gap in the traffic, and they moved off, the two men exchanged something, the shorter man passing something to the gentleman who looked exactly like Lord Audley-Sinclair. Both men checked that they had not been watched before melting into the darkness.

Lottie wondered what mischief or deceit the Lord was up to because she had no doubt that he was deceitful with ulterior motives. Lottie had read, in Amelia's own words, that the Lord was taking care of her and would also take care of the baby when it was born imminently.

Amelia wrote that his Lordship had found Amelia lodgings in the west of the city, where there was a walled garden and beautiful views of the Royal Windsor Park. There was a library where she could read to her heart's content, and she had found a copy of Shakespeare's *Romeo and Juliet*, her favourite book, in Italian, which she loved. She even quoted a passage in her letter, which Lottie's lips stumbled over.

Amelia's letters to her aunt spoke of the Lord's goodness, his open heart, and dedication to the care and safety of her and the unborn child. Surely, it was his duty after almost ruining Amelia's reputation as the father of Amelia's child.

Lottie had yet to see any of those traits in the man, and she did not understand the high esteem in which Amelia held him, her adoration for the scoundrel obvious.

In Lottie's short acquaintance of Lord Audley-Sinclair, with what she had witnessed and experienced herself, he had the nerve to come to Lady Eleanor's funeral, without bringing her niece or their child. Had he kept Amelia away from her family after the birth, kept their child hidden? Was he ashamed of Amelia and their child? Did he find them an encumbrance to his philandering lifestyle, his womanising ways?

Lottie desired nothing more than to challenge him to tell her the truth, but she could not challenge him without giving herself away if he did not know already. Was a future that she was not actually entitled to any more important than finding out about the past of the girl she was masquerading as? There was only one way to find out.

Chapter 9

Nathaniel was late to the Freshford ball, not unusual in the slightest; in fact, it was almost expected, but for once it was completely unplanned. He wanted to be in situ at the ball when the guests arrived so that he could observe Miss Amelia Colton to see if she would give herself away without his intervention.

Since his sources had told him Miss Colton was in residence at the Freshford Estate, as the guest of the Duke and Duchess Antcliffe, she had been in his thoughts, most of the time unwanted. Against his will, he was impressed with how far up the pecking order this imposter had risen in so short of a time. But he knew without a shadow of a doubt that she was an imposter.

During his most recent venture, which started with a clandestine meeting in a park in Bath in the dark of night with a man of no name and ended with a midnight ride deep into the Somerset countryside to retrieve a valuable document, Amelia, or whatever she was called, was often on his mind.

He had pondered the reason for her pretence, the end goal of masquerading as Amelia, and he could only draw one conclusion. Money.

That in itself was no surprise, for what marriage was ever for anything less than wealth, be that money or property. If not a father needing to prevent the passing of his worldly goods to a male heir, some second cousin thrice removed, instead of his daughters, then a young, impoverished widow in need of a rich husband to keep her in the lifestyle to which she had become accustomed.

Nathaniel had all the information he needed to expose her, just his word was enough. To do so would likely cost him dearly, both personally and professionally. Better he do what he was good at, although he did not usually employ such tactics with the women he took as lovers.

His work was dangerous, and what he knew about leading members of the government, society, and royalty, both in England and on the Continent, could start a revolution. He used subterfuge and lies, observations and whispers, darkness and dingy corners as the tools of his trade. While his reputation was notorious, it also provided him cover. If people wanted to gossip about his womanising and bad behaviour, so be it.

The attention kept the two most important things in his life secret, his important work and the child who became his ward the moment her mother died in childbirth seven years before. Because the mother was the real Amelia Colton, because he drew his own fingertips over her eyelids in the minutes after her passing, he knew the woman was imitating Amelia.

Nathaniel moved among his acquaintances at the ball, going through the motions of meeting and greeting, flirting and fawning, but his eyes followed Miss Amelia Colton wherever she went.

Now, as the Master of Ceremonies, a familiar face on the Bath social calendar, announced his arrival at the Freshford ball, he could not necessarily use those same tools as he went about his business. His late arrival however, went largely unnoticed, such was the gaiety of the several hundred guests, allowing him close access to places where secrets lived.

As he leaned against a marble pillar near the entrance to the ladies' salon, he heard the catty whispers of the society women about the newcomer, one Amelia Colton.

"I heard tell she has been working abroad as the governess for an ambassador in one of the small European principalities."

Nathaniel smiled to himself. He had started that very rumour seven years ago when Amelia had first called upon him for help. She had indeed spent a few months overseas as the companion to a countess who wanted to travel to Lourdes to take the Holy Water and then on to recuperate at the Italian lakes.

How short the collective memory was.

"Indeed. There was also talk of an engagement to an elderly Italian count, who died before they could marry."

The two women clucked like hens in a coop, but he knew before the evening was out, the stories would have spread and likely changed to be even more extravagant. He would store the gossip for possible later use, depending on how he decided to handle her unmasking.

Two of the three Miss Hayes, out in society, led a group of young women from the salon, and Nathaniel ducked behind a portly dowager to avoid discovery. As used to interrogation as he was from his time on the battlefields of Europe, there was nothing as terrifying as the inquisition from a group of marrying-age girls, who all saw him as the perfect catch.

If the two Hayes girls were present, that meant Miss Daniella Hayes, their sister, would likely be in attendance with her fiancée, his good friend, Lord Barnaby Westeroy. Neatly avoiding yet another group of women on the hunt, he spied Barnaby dancing with Daniella, and he thought what a handsome couple they made. Daniella was beautiful and a little shy upon first knowing her, but utterly pleasant and a calming influence on Barney.

Instead, he looked around the huge room, searching for Amelia, and happened upon Lady Anne Gilroy, deep in conversation with some of the local gentry. Nathaniel remembered this was her hometown. She would, of course, know practically everyone, given that she had been able to maintain some sort of status after that unpleasant business with her late husband.

Unable to find Amelia, he decided to take in some fresh air, the mix of perfumes, colognes, and flowers mingling heavily. A group of women gathered on the terrace, overlooking the moonlit grounds, talking animatedly, as their chaperones lurked in the doorways, keeping an eye on their charges. Miss Arabella Hayes was holding court, and Nathaniel recognised the distinct signs of a predator going in for the kill, her gaze honed on her prey, a smile on her face, aware of what was about to happen.

Nathaniel moved closer so that he could hear Arabella steer the conversation to travel and foreign languages.

"I hated learning French, such a painful language. Nowhere near as pretty as Italian," Arabella opined loudly, stepping into the centre of the circle.

Her sister, Francesca, as curvaceous as her mother and just about as flirtatious, seconded the opinion.

"And what of you, Miss Colton?" Arabella gave a friendly smile, as she singled out the girl in the midnight blue silk. "How many languages do you speak, having spent so much time abroad? I hear tell that you are very well travelled."

All eyes turned to the girl pretending to be Amelia Colton, and Nathaniel recognised the panic in her widening eyes. The girl looked from Arabella to Francesca to the rest of the group, and he wondered if she was about to bolt as her shoulders started to round, her confidence almost deserting her. He would be heartily content to see the imposter caught out in a lie, even if the lie was pure gossip and utterly unfounded.

He watched, suddenly enjoying himself at the prospect of humiliation in front of a group of her supposed peers, when he saw the girl change in front of his eyes. Her head lifted, her shoulders pushed back, and she opened her mouth, her words striking a chord that had been silent for some time.

"Il mio unico amore è scaturito dal mio unico odio, visto troppo presto sconosciuto e conosciuto troppo tardi!"

(My only love sprung from my only hate, seen too soon unknown, and known too late!)

It was a quote from Shakespeare's *Romeo and Juliet* that Amelia learned by heart and used to recite in the garden of the Windsor house he bought for her. Slightly shaken by hearing the words again, Nathaniel stepped forward, his presence parting the circle of women around Amelia; however, her back was turned to him as she addressed Arabella.

"Per me è una nascita prodigiosa dell'amore."

(Prodigious birth of love is it to me.)

As he spoke, Amelia turned to face him, and she looked at him hard, and then her face softened as she continued. The irony of the entire verse was not lost on him.

"Che devo amare un nemico odiato."

(That I must love a loathed enemy.) This girl was clearly a good study, and she completed the passage passingly well for someone who most likely had never been to Italy, let alone learned the language.

Some in the gathered group began to clap, entranced by the performance. Nathaniel would not have been surprised if Amelia had taken a bow, but he was the only one who knew the truth.

Arabella at first looked furious as her plan to embarrass Amelia had backfired, peeved that her apparent rival had risen to her challenge so beautifully, and quickly rearranged her features to look delighted to see him. Her sister, with less experience and less subtlety but much more ingenuity, pinched her cheeks and pulled down on her skirt to improve her décolletage.

The master of disguise, if only masking his disdain for Amelia, Nathaniel entertained the crowd with enthusiastic flattery and suggestively inappropriate comments. If one had been looking closely enough, he revealed glimpses of his clandestine life, his ability to change depending on the situation, but the girls were too enamoured to notice, all but one gazing dreamily at him, their eyes round and shiny as they imagined becoming Lady Audley-Sinclair.

At Nathaniel's next bawdy joke, more suitable to a tavern full of gentleman than a group of young debutantes, chaperones descended to reclaim their complaining charges. Only Lady Anne remained at a discreet distance.

"Thank you, my Lord, for your part in the conversation. It was unnecessary, however, I'm sure it had the desired effect on your captive audience." Amelia curtsied.

"My pleasure, Miss Colton," he replied softly. "Don't get too far out of your depth again. I will not be there to rescue you next time."

Over Amelia's shoulder, he saw Sir James Holden, the eternal Bachelor of Bath as he was unkindly known, hovering, as was his wont with pretty unattached young ladies. The man clearly had designs on Amelia, no doubt encouraged by Lady Anne, who joined up with him, and they were headed for Amelia.

"Lady Anne, Sir James, good evening." Nathaniel bowed, before nodding to Amelia. "Miss Colton, *buona notte*."

Something flared in Amelia's eyes, and Nathaniel knew he had scored a point in the game they were playing together. But he had other duties to perform, such as the most eligible man at the ball.

He had no intention of patronising Miss Colton with a dance, which would speak volumes amongst the assembled guests who had also been at the recent balls in London. Instead, he flirted and danced with as many women as he could, hoping that Amelia, probably stuck with Sir James if Lady Anne had anything to do with it, felt his slight with every new partner he took on the dance floor.

But, as much as he tried to avoid it, the imposter drew his attention, for she was just as popular as he. Amelia's gaze sought him out, dancing away when their eyes met. The girl was interested in him, even if she did not know it. Or if she knew it, she resented the attraction.

What fun he could have with her, parry and riposte, hide and seek, the hunter and the prey, over the coming weeks, with balls and gatherings littering the social calendar in Bath and London. But business would take him to the Continent in the coming days, and he could not risk any entanglement, delay, or distraction, no matter how surprisingly attractive the proposition.

Chapter 10

Lottie returned home to Ringwood, glad to be back where she did not have to hide behind a story, pretending to be someone else.

Although she had fun with Freya and her girls and enjoyed meeting new people, it was tiring trying to keep things straight in her mind, remembering what she had said before. Being at home was safe and secure. She could be herself around Holmes and Maggie; there was no need for airs and graces.

Lottie wanted to help out around the house, as that was her real position in life, but without Lady Eleanor to tend to, there wasn't enough work to go around.

By this time, she had read all of Amelia's letters several times over, in case she missed anything, but she was still not in possession of the whole story. The letters had stopped abruptly, just a few weeks before the expected birth of her child, and Lottie imagined all matter of different endings to Amelia's story.

What if the child had not survived its birth, and Amelia was inconsolable with grief, driven mad by her loss? Had Lord Audley-Sinclair had her committed because he couldn't stand the wailing sorrow from the attic room where he had banished her?

Perhaps the Lord had married Amelia out of necessity before she gave birth, and she now lived her life in leisure, just her and her child? They would want for nothing, for Freya and Lady Anne had spoken of both the family's historic wealth and his own private income which came about by nefarious means.

Had he hidden them both out of sight and out of mind so that he could continue to live his life however he pleased?

Lottie might never know it all, but in her letters, Amelia was consistently certain in one thing, that Lord Audley-Sinclair was looking after her extremely well.

As spring turned to summer, Lottie took long walks on the manor's grounds, often straying outside of the boundary walls into the very edges of the New Forest. She looked forward to the weekly missive from Freya, who wrote of the happenings in Bath and London, rueing her friend's absence due to Lady Anne's prolonged illness, which kept her bedridden for over a month. This meant that Lottie, without a chaperone, was unable to attend any social gatherings to which she had been invited.

Life returned to a gentle rhythm but Lottie, having had a glimpse of the glittering glamour of society balls, having worn the dresses made of luxurious silk, having rubbed shoulders with the highest of society, found herself restless. So much so that when she returned one afternoon from one of her long walks, she was ridiculously pleased to find Lady Anne waiting impatiently in the library for her.

"Where have you been?" Lady Anne barked, her voice a little hoarse, a handkerchief pressed to the corner of her mouth. "You look like you've been dragged through a hedge backwards, my girl."

"I am pleased to see you are recovered, my Lady." Lottie hid her smile as she curtsied.

No matter what they might plot and play at, the woman was still a Lady, and Lottie was not.

"Appearances can be deceiving, as well you know, young lady." She coughed delicately into her handkerchief and took a sip of tea that Maggie had provided her. "I rallied myself sufficiently to make the difficult journey here before travelling on to London in a day or so."

Lottie's stomach flipped slightly in anticipation, but she was unsure why.

"Do you require company, my Lady?"

"What I require is money, to be blunt. Funds to pay for my ongoing recovery. My own doctor has referred me to an eminent physician from India, who has a practice in the City. He considers it a vital part of my rehabilitation from this frightful disease. I am far too ill to be gallivanting after you from one frivolous party to another. Who knows how long it will take to recover."

Lady Anne swooned back against the cushions on the chaise, and her eyelids fluttered shut as she groaned and coughed, spluttered and moaned.

Lottie was unmoved and simply watched the performance from her front-row seat. When no comfort or pity was forthcoming, Lady Anne lifted one eyelid to see what her audience of one was doing.

"Lady Anne, our agreement does not allow for extraneous funds. We are bound, surely, by the original terms?" Lottie's voice was polite, but firm.

Of course, Lottie would not deny another human, even Lady Anne, the care they needed to regain their health, but neither would she acquiesce without assurance of something in return.

Lady Anne sniffed or scoffed, Lottie was not sure which, but she was sure the woman knew she was going to have to rethink her plan.

"You may travel with me to London as my companion. I may be well enough in time to make introductions to several suitable matches." Lottie could not keep the smile from her face, but Lady Anne narrowed her eyes. "Know that my health comes before your social life, my girl."

"Of course, my Lady," Lottie said deferentially and stood. "May I refresh your drink? Or would you prefer to retire before dinner, given your long journey from Bath today?"

"Indeed," Lady Anne nodded, satisfied, but Lottie was sure she had the better end of the deal.

With Lady Anne otherwise engaged with her treatments, Lottie would surely have some freedom to explore the city, visit shops or museums, or take afternoon tea. Yes, she was sure to have one or two opportunities, as long as she avoided the part of town where she spent the first years of her life. Nothing would get her back to Cheapside and the slums from which she had run.

***

Lottie shivered, almost a week later, even though the sun shone brightly, its heat warming the carriage through the glass.

Lady Anne had been vague as to their final destination in the City, and Lottie knew why as they travelled into one of the poorer parts of London, one that she knew well from her childhood.

Memories poured over her like ice water, unpleasant smells hit her nose, and she watched the women going about their business, from those selling flowers to cover the stench to those selling their wares to any man who would have her. Lottie shrank back into the plush seat of the carriage, desperately hoping not to recognise her mother among them.

Lady Anne, her malaise distinctly improving the nearer they got to the end of their journey, was almost giddy with excitement, a pink tinge colouring her cheeks, and Lottie was glad one of them was looking forward to their time there.

The mysterious doctor had left word for them at the coaching inn they stopped at last evening that he had rented rooms for the two ladies in a boarding house. Now that Lottie knew where they were headed, she had no doubt that the boarding house would not be up to the standard that both she and Lady Anne were used to.

The carriage turned through an archway and into the inner courtyard of a tavern with boarding accommodation above. As the coachman and his groom struggled to retrieve their luggage from the roof of the carriage, Lottie followed as Lady Anne, her handkerchief doused in scent once more at her nose, led the way into the tavern to speak with the owner.

The tavern was dark, the floor sticky with spilled drink, the air thick with tobacco smoke, and the landlord greeted them with a lascivious grin. Lady Anne stoutly ignored the appreciative looks and catcalls from the patrons as she followed a serving girl up narrow stairs.

Lottie knew the girl could not have been much older than she was herself when she ran from this place, was almost pinned to the spot by the past, but forced herself to follow. Where Lady Anne's gaze stayed straight ahead, her nose in the air, Lottie's eyes darted from left to right, wondering if she knew anyone or if they knew her.

There, in a dark corner, whispering to another man over a flagon of ale, was Lord Audley-Sinclair. Their gaze slid around corners to make sure their secrets were safe, and Lottie hurried up the stairs before his eyes fell upon her.

Whatever he was doing there, although surely shady, had to be a pure coincidence. When one ventured into the London slums, one was sure to find a certain type of character such as he, in a certain type of location such as this.

Lady Anne, unable to wait until the following day to attend the doctor's clinic, generously tipped the serving girl to unpack the trunks in their adjoining rooms and ordered the carriage to meet them out the front of the tavern to take them directly there.

Lottie thought about feigning tiredness, but she doubted Lady Anne had the experience nor, frankly, the wit to deal with any unwelcome attention from the inhabitants of Cheapside. Although it had been some years since she had survived by herself, she would be able to handle certain situations better than her chaperone.

The stairs took them directly to the entrance to the tavern, so Lottie was able to exit the building without any chance of Lord Audley-Sinclair spotting her if he was even still there. The short journey would have been quicker on foot but would have increased the risk of Lady Anne catching some other ailment from the dirty streets and the filthy dank air.

Lottie tried to wait patiently while Lady Anne took her treatment; however, her thoughts of Lord Audley-Sinclair and his secrets made her fidgety. Combined with the thick, sweet incense burning on every surface, she was desperate for air, no matter how rank.

"Milady, I beg your pardon, but I must take leave. I am feeling quite overwhelmed by the business of the city," Lottie whispered through the curtain that separated the doctor's waiting area from his treatment room.

She thought that Lady Anne might refuse to be treated in such undignified surroundings, but she was enthusiastic about everything.

"Of course, my dear girl." Her chaperone's voice floated through the thin material. "Return safely, and I will see you at dinner."

Lottie was glad to be out of the heady atmosphere and was amazed at how much she could remember of the area, slipping easily into alleyways and shortcuts she had thought long forgotten. She was about to turn one final time to take her to the tavern when she saw dark curls just peeping out from under a man's hat. It was Lord Audley-Sinclair.

She knew she should not linger in the side streets, let alone follow the Lord, but she could not let this opportunity pass. He might lead her to Amelia, even if such an event would certainly end her own pretence.

Lottie was already garnering unwanted attention from the locals in her fine hat and no doubt stood out like a sore thumb. Well-dressed ladies did not frequent this part of town, and so she needed to make a change. Thankfully, her cape was plain enough, but she deftly removed her hat, giving it to a passing crone who cackled her thanks. Lottie tied her large white handkerchief about her head, just like she had when she worked as a scullery maid when she was a child, now much less conspicuous.

She followed the Lord as he strolled through the streets of the slum, clearly in no hurry. She was forced to slow her pace painfully as he stopped to pass the time of day openly with several market stall-holders, and Lottie was surprised at how comfortable he appeared with the lowest classes in society.

Lottie almost walked into Lord Audley-Sinclair as he stood at the side of the road to look at his pocket watch. She ducked behind a pillar, her breath coming fast and shallow at the very real chance of being discovered.

Shortly, a grand carriage pulled up at the kerb, and the person inside dropped the window as the Lord stepped closer. Lottie could make out a man wearing a powder wig in the carriage, but their conversation was quick and quiet. Whoever the individual was, he appeared very wealthy, given the heavy golden rings on his hand as he gave Lord Audley-Sinclair a thick leather wallet, containing who knew what.

As quickly as it arrived, the coach departed, and the Lord tucked the wallet inside his coat and carried on his way.

Lottie knew it was dangerous to follow him any further as the afternoon turned later. Lady Anne was likely to return to the tavern soon if she had not already, and Lottie would have to explain her absence.

Alone in her room a short while later, with Lady Anne snoring contentedly in her own chamber, Lottie pondered on her adventure and what she had seen.

What had the wallet contained? Jewels, money, secrets? Paying for the Lord's assistance or his service? Lottie had heard talk of dangerous missions for powerful men, witnessed firsthand whispered conversations in the dead of the night in parks and in dimly lit taverns—he was indeed a man of secrets.

Lottie wondered if his rakish reputation was a mask, concealing a deeper purpose. Perhaps the letters from Amelia's own hand held the truth, that he was, in fact, a good man, involved in secret things. How on earth would she get to the heart of this tale without confronting him?

Chapter 11

Lottie and Lady Anne fell into a routine whereby Lottie would accompany her on her visit to the physician every other day, often late morning, after which the older woman would be exhausted and need to rest.

This gave Lottie the freedom she had been hoping for, and she often spent several hours walking through Cheapside, wearing a worn dress that she had exchanged with one of the barmaids in the tavern. Even though Lottie had become accustomed to dressing well, she had spent many years in poor-quality, ill-fitting clothing, especially as a child.

While she had no desire to return to feeling the rough, loosely woven material against her skin, she was not completely uncomfortable in the attire. It allowed her to blend in, to move almost unseen, as she searched for Lord Audley-Sinclair. She had also paid Lizzie, the young serving girl, to let her know of any *toffs*, as the girl called them, who frequented the tavern.

Despite her best efforts, Lottie had seen neither hide nor hair of the elusive Lord since her first day in Cheapside. She knew it would be like trying to find a freckle on a frog in a city the size of London.

Tired of the grime of the slum, Lottie hailed a cab to take her to wherever was greenest in the vicinity, and grinning, the driver took her money and headed for Brunswick Square Gardens in Bloomsbury. Lottie wondered if the area was as eponymous as Cheapside and would have wildflower meadows as far as the eye could see.

Upon her arrival, she was only mildly disappointed that there were no meadows. However, she was used to the green grounds at Ringwood Manor, and Lottie was delighted to see a large green field with grand townhouses lining its edges.

She spent a very pleasant hour exploring the smaller garden squares in the surrounding streets, saving the largest space for last. The uniformity of its planting and trees spoke of a curated space, rather than a natural occurrence, but nonetheless, Lottie was able to breathe freely for the first time in two weeks.

Without the pressure of searching out the errant Lord, Lottie sat on a wrought iron bench in the shade of a sweet chestnut tree and enjoyed the warmth of the afternoon sun.

Her thoughts wandered aimlessly as she watched governesses marching school-age children briskly along the paths that criss-crossed the field and elderly well-born ladies taking an afternoon stroll. A lone male, striding purposefully along the path, swinging his cane before each step, caught her eye. His gait was familiar, although he moved with more speed than he had when she followed him two weeks before.

Lottie watched rapt as she projected the direction of his travel. A woman with a young girl noticed the interloper, and the child ran towards him with alacrity. She stopped short and curtsied, and he, Lord Nathaniel Audley-Sinclair, bowed deeply to the little girl, and then bent one knee in order to catch her as she threw herself bodily into his arms.

The innocence and sincerity of the embrace reminded Lottie of how the Duke was with his three daughters, and a lump formed in her throat.

Could this be Amelia's child? Is the woman now walking toward the Lord and the little girl Amelia herself?

The woman curtsied, and the Lord nodded his head. The exchange seemed polite but formal, and Lottie did not imagine any overt connection between the two adults. In fact, the little girl awkwardly linked her arm with the Lord's, and they strolled slowly for some time, seemingly deep in conversation. Several times over, the little girl gesticulated with both hands and seemed to be rebuked gently by the woman, who walked a little distance behind them.

Lottie knew this was the perfect opportunity to trail Lord Audley-Sinclair. She might never have the chance again and was determined to stay with him wherever he went. When the Lord bent to press a kiss to the child's forehead, the lump of emotion returned, and for a moment, Lottie's eyes misted over with tears.

In that time, the Lord turned and began to head directly in her direction, and she scrambled, in a most unladylike manner, up from the bench, and thrust herself into a bush behind the large sweet chestnut tree, for she could not be sure in which direction he would pass her by.

He passed closely enough for Lottie to smell his cologne, the same scent she remembered from dancing with him, the same scent that lingered in the library at Ringwood Manor after he had left.

Although she followed at a distance so as not to be seen, the Lord walked quickly, moving with confidence and vigour. Lottie was not familiar with this part of the city, even though it was but a few miles from Cheapside, where she grew up.

Much as the time before, she followed him along clean, wide streets, around corners, up steps, through a maze of white stone and red brick buildings, a far cry from the wooden ones in the slums. The area reminded Lottie of Bath, and she spent just a moment too long looking up at her surroundings, that the Lord disappeared from view.

Lottie looked left and right and saw only one place where he could have gone. She hurried across the street and around the corner into what appeared to be a dead end. But she found an almost hidden archway, just out of view, and slipped through that, only to find herself at the centre of five different pathways.

She picked one and she found herself face to face with Lord Audley-Sinclair.

"Miss Colton, what a coincidence we should meet in the back streets of Holborn."

He smiled widely, as if pleased to see her, but his eyes were cold and bore into her.

"My Lord," Lottie breathed the words but could find no other to explain what she was doing here.

He took a step closer, and she backed away again, as if they were dancing once more in the ballroom at the Star and Garter. Lottie did not remember him being so very tall or his shoulders so very wide.

She felt the solidity of a wall at her back, and her heart pounded to be in such close proximity to this man, unchaperoned, unobserved. Lottie felt a warmth swathing her entire body, from the backs of her knees to the small of her back. Her chest, her throat, and her cheeks were surely flaming red with the shame of being caught red-handed.

Lottie's breathing became shallow, and she felt as if she might faint from lack of air. It was all she could do to watch as he bowed his head, moved his mouth next to her ear so close she could feel the warmth of his breath as he whispered to her.

"Are you in need of rescuing once more, Miss Colton?"

She remembered his act of kindness at the Freshford ball, when he interceded in the conversation that Miss Arabella Hayes had turned on Lottie, calling her out about the story that she had been a governess in Europe and knew several languages. Luckily, Lottie had found the quote in one of Amelia's letters to her aunt and had loved the way the Italian words felt in her mouth.

But his behaviour this day was assuredly not kind, as he pressed himself closer to her, closer than when they had danced the waltz. That was in public, where propriety dictated the amount of space between their bodies. There appeared to be no such propriety here and now.

The same spirit of survival that flooded her body when challenged by Arabella returned with gusto, and Lottie felt no compunction in making her discomfort known, even if her body was reacting treacherously to the closeness of his Lordship.

"Lord Audley-Sinclair," Lottie said, meeting his gaze as she put one hand on his shoulder and took his hand in hers, as if they were about to dance.

Somewhat taken aback, Lottie was able to leverage some room by pushing forward and turning slightly so that they faced each other in the passageway.

The Lord grinned, and his gaze raked over Lottie's body, leaving her feeling exposed, even naked. His behaviour was truly beyond the pale.

"As you are so keen to dance, my Lord, I will gladly save every first dance for the remainder of the season just for you." Lottie's words were bold, brazen even, for a young lady did not ask a gentleman to dance.

Lord Audley-Sinclair's gaze settled on Lottie's upturned face, for she would not break eye contact with such a man again. He seemed to study her, his expression impenetrable, so she was unable to guess at his thoughts.

"Whatever you are doing, Miss Colton, whatever it is you hope to achieve, I would counsel you to think twice before continuing." His voice was low, warning.

"You would forbid me from taking an afternoon constitutional while my chaperone, Lady Anne Gilroy, rests after taking medical treatment for what ails her?"

Lottie clasped her hands behind her back, and the Lord's gaze dropped momentarily as the movement drew his attention.

"You are a child in a man's war, young lady. Your carefully woven world could come unravelled at any point. A gentle tug on a loose thread, and you will be undone."

"Do you mean to threaten me, sir?" Lottie's pride and fighting spirit simmered just below the surface of her thinly worn patience.

She had not survived a tough life in the slums, running away from everything she knew to find something better. She was rescued by Holmes and brought to Lady Gilroy by sheer chance. She knew how to take the opportunities that presented themselves, and she could give as good as she got. Even if her opponent was a very wealthy, very powerful, and very attractive man.

"Tread carefully, sir," she said softly. "I may be young, but I know enough. I know about you."

His blue eyes flashed dangerously, like a dagger of ice slicing through her soul, and Lottie knew she had hit upon a very raw nerve. One that was hidden away in London from prying eyes. Lottie knew the truth now, that the girl in the park was Amelia's daughter. His daughter.

As the missing pieces of Amelia's story fell into place, Lottie expected the man to back away, to back down. But he did not.

The Lord reached out for her, putting his hands none too gently on her arms, pulled her roughly to him and kissed her thoroughly. It was all she could do not to faint into his arms, as she felt all the air leaving her body, her head as light as a cloud.

This was what it felt like, more than she had imagined, and yet—

Lottie remembered belatedly that this was utterly inappropriate, that his actions were unwanted, and she pushed against him with all her might. No delicate dance steps required in a situation such as this. She slapped his face wholeheartedly, and instead of giving an apology, he grinned.

Lord Audley-Sinclair stepped back and looked her up and down almost appreciatively, and Lottie felt even more insulted.

"We both have secrets, Miss Colton. Let's make a deal. I'll keep yours if you keep mine."

His audacity left her almost as speechless as his kiss had left her breathless.

"Until next time, *Amelia*."

Chapter 12

Nathaniel's ward, the beautiful Arya, was the most fragile of all his secrets and the one he would protect at all costs. The child's laughter echoed through the house as her governess chased her, begging her to get ready for bed. Her joy and innocence echoed in the corridors of his heart long after the sounds faded, as the little girl was readied for sleep.

He had never loved anyone or anything as wholeheartedly as he did Arya. When he had sworn to Amelia on her deathbed that he would look after her until she came of age, he had no concept of what that actually meant, not truly.

He was rich enough for the girl to have the very best of everything, and money was no object. But what use was money when a baby's teeth were coming in, and the exhausted nurse had desperately asked him one night to take the baby for just a short while? That very night was the moment of his epiphany when he knew this defenceless babe would have his heart for the rest of his life.

Arya was now six years old, and Nathaniel had kept her true identity secret for this long. He made sure they were very rarely seen in public together. But could he continue to keep her safe now that this girl, who was definitely not Miss Amelia Colton, apparently knew the truth? How she had made the connection was beyond his knowledge at this moment, but he would do whatever was necessary to find out.

Nathaniel was secure in the girl's safety. The people who looked after her, he would entrust his life to. His household staff would be loyal to him and Arya to the ends of the earth, and her governess was the same woman who had looked after him and his brother as children, who would also lay down her life if he asked her.

In his study, before heading out for the evening, Nathaniel took another glance at a letter hand delivered not an hour. He had cast it aside in anger as soon as he opened it, when the subject of the message became clear. Reading it again, only marginally calmer, it appeared that Arya's sire—Nathaniel would not grace the scoundrel with the title of father—had recently re-entered the London social scene after years of debauchery in Marrakech, for the entirety of Arya's life.

Sir Douglas Shepherd had disgraced Amelia, first by being intimate with her outside of wedlock, and secondly by refusing to honour the situation in which she found herself, with child. When Shepherd had discovered that Nathaniel was a family friend of Amelia's and would likely bring the world down around his ears for his appalling behaviour, he skedaddled out of the capital and out of the country as fast as his knock-kneed, lily-livered, weak-willed body would carry him.

Yes, Shepherd and Nathaniel had yet to cross paths, but it would be inevitable that they would.

Arriving at Almack's later that evening, after drinks with Barney at his gentlemen's club in Soho, Nathaniel was in a surprisingly jovial mood as he was announced. He took the time to stop and pass a moment with many more people than normal, flirting with the ladies and flattering the gentleman. Until he happened across an incongruous sight.

Lady Anne was deep in conversation, which happened quite publicly at a gathering at Almack's. Nathaniel was surprised to see Sir Douglas Shepherd there, as well as Miss Amelia Colton.

As yet, they were not moving within the same circle of guests, and he supposed that the whole evening might pass just so.

The Almack was very particular in its segregation of the highest, the high, and the not quite high enough. Miss Colton, as an apparent newcomer to the social scene, was very much on the edges or lower rung of the hierarchy. Shepherd, despite his atrocities to dear Amelia, was the son of an Earl, who so far had refused to die and let his errant offspring lead the family and, therefore, was able to float between the highs and the lows with ease, much like Nathaniel.

However, that was without taking into consideration the most determined way that Lady Anne was introducing her ward to every high-born male she came across. Nathaniel saw Lady Anne turn her attention to her next opportunity, her sharp features reminding him of a bird of prey. Her gaze alighted on Shepherd, and after the woman had checked to see if Miss Colton was still engaged in conversation, Lady Anne steered her towards the man who had ruined Amelia's life.

Nathaniel watched cautiously as Lady Anne introduced the two for any sign of recognition from Shepherd at the mention of Amelia's name. He also observed Miss Colton closely, knowing full well that she would have no idea who this man was because she was not really Amelia. Although Shepherd was rapt with attention at the pretty young woman before him—she did look very fetching in a dark crimson gown—there was no sign that he had met her before.

Shepherd bowed deeply and glanced pointedly at the dance floor, where couples were assembling for the next dance. Lady Anne's enthusiastic squawk of a response could be heard clearly in Mayfair.

"Verily, Sir Shepherd, you are too, too kind. To dance with such a fine gentleman would be simply divine."

Nathaniel could almost imagine Lady Anne was speaking about herself, and yet she pushed Miss Colton forward with a very firm hand on the small of her back. The two danced, Shepherd with a lecherous grin on his shiny red face, Miss Colton with a polite but fixed smile on hers, her teeth clenched tightly.

As they stepped through the movements, Shepherd tried to hold her hand more tightly, but she offered only her very fingertips, and it seemed to Nathaniel that she was keen to get away from his sweaty clutches. When the music ended, Miss Colton bobbed a curtsy and pulled her hand from Shepherd's while he bowed, turning gratefully to another suitor, Sir James Holden who had been waiting in the wings eagerly.

So it went for the next three dances; each suitor older and more excited than the last to dance with the young woman, and she with the lockjaw smile, for fear of seeming impolite and ungrateful.

Instead of taking pleasure in her displeasure, Nathaniel pondered if he should rescue her again. If Shepherd weren't so in his cups, pacing up and down the edge of the dance floor, waiting for his chance to reclaim Miss Colton for his own, with a drink in each hand, he might put two and two together, and realise that this wasn't her, not the Amelia he had known. He could expose her, and Nathaniel could not let that happen, for then his secret would naturally unfurl.

Nathaniel swept in and took Miss Colton in his arms, without formal greeting nor question, to dance the waltz for the third time at such an event. Such a bold, possessive move, he knew, would set tongues wagging. He acted as if he and Miss Colton were much closer than they were, but appearances were deceiving.

"I saved the first dance for you, sir. Your presumption that I wish to dance with you now is ill-placed." Miss Colton's voice was cold, and her eyes colder, and yet her cheeks flamed, with what he was unsure.

"We are sufficiently acquainted, Miss Colton, to know of each other's secrets. You should also know that I pay no consequence to what is expected of me."

"You will not be insulted then if I leave the dance this instance."

The girl started to turn in his arms, her hand twisting out of his hold, the gap between them widening quickly. Nathaniel was aware of everyone's intense interest in them, along with the hovering husbands-in-waiting, and could imagine the fuss that would follow if she left him standing, and what it might do to his reputation. He would become the focus of societal storytelling, attract unnecessary attention when he needed the veil of anonymity for his work.

"Do you have such little regard for the consequences of your own actions, Miss Colton?"

Nathaniel looked down at her upturned face, her eyes widening for a moment.

"When you started this charade, did you think any further than a fine husband? If you leave now, who will you engage next, Sir Shepherd or Sir Holden? Or someone else?"

He left the question hanging, and they danced in silence for three more dances until the ballroom buzzed with gossip, and the young woman grasped his arm with both hands, holding tightly as if she were about to swoon.

He took one look at her pale face, her wide eyes, and recognised how tired she was and possibly weak with hunger.

"Forgive me," Nathaniel said under his breath, and carefully put his arm around her waist, holding her against him as they walked toward a private room where a buffet was laid out on a long table.

"Do not trouble yourself," Amelia urged. "I have already taken far too much of your time this evening, sir."

Nathaniel scoffed as he dropped her a little unceremoniously onto a chaise before pouring a glass of water from a carafe and giving it to her.

She drank gladly and emptied the drink in one go, handing the glass back to him. He tried not to smile, turning quickly so she would not see his amusement. He poured another glass, nodded to a waiting servant to serve the young lady from the buffet.

"Stay here, Miss Colton. I have a brief item of business to complete. Eat, rest, and I will return momentarily."

He stalked out of the room, nearly colliding with Shepherd as he cannoned off a pillar, but the drunken reprobate could wait. Nathaniel's business was with Lady Anne. He found her deep in gossip, carefully hidden with fans and whispers, and did not hesitate to catch her attention.

"My Lady, may I take a moment of your time? I have an important matter I wish to consult you on."

Lady Anne exchanged a knowing look with her peers, who watched with bated breath as she stepped out of their circle.

"Lord Audley-Sinclair, you flatter me with your kind attention this evening, both to me and my ward, Amel—"

He cut the woman off with a look before he said his piece.

"I know your ward is not Amelia Colton, madam. I know this because I witnessed her death seven years ago. I know not to what end either you or your ward are working, nor do I care. I will keep the girl's secret as long as she stays away from London. I am sure there are suitors aplenty in Bath or Winchester who will make a willing husband."

"My Lord?" The woman had the nerve to look shocked, but he was not moved.

"My Lady. I would advise strongly against propagating a marriage for your ward with either Sir Anthony Shepherd or Sir James Holden. Both are too old and too set in their ways to make a suitable match."

Lady Anne eyed Nathaniel, then tilted her head a little too coquettishly for his liking.

"For the sake of Amelia—" Lady Anne paused as Nathaniel glared at her. "—my ward, I will keep Sir Holden company, persuade him to angle his affections elsewhere. This will no doubt smooth the path for anyone else who may have designs on her."

Nathaniel certainly did not like the inference that anyone else might be him.

"Of course, my Lord, entertaining a gentleman such as Sir Holden does not come without expense."

Nathaniel thought Amelia, whoever she is, could do a lot better without Lady Anne to counsel her. The woman, widowed and single for far too long, had become almost mercenary in her endeavours and clearly did not have Amelia's or anyone's best interests at heart, only her own.

"I will arrange for a small stipend to be paid to you, my Lady, for your efforts."

Nathaniel bowed, ending any further discussion with the insufferable woman. He pitied Amelia for the choices she had made, but her cards would fall as fate decreed. In his line of work, he knew to keep his enemies closer than his friends, so he would keep Amelia close until such a time he could safely unmask her and reveal her true intentions.

When that might be, he did not know, but he would be prepared, come what may.

Chapter 13

Lottie strolled behind Lady Anne as they walked along the Royal Avenue, enjoying the late June sunshine. Out of her chaperone's sphere, even a few paces, Lottie felt like a bird released from its cage.

Since the Almack ball, Lady Anne had been overtly attentive, at Lottie's side for the majority of her waking hours, in London, at Ringwood Manor, and for the past fortnight, as her guest at her apartment in Bath.

The accommodations in Bath were compact but comfortable, yet it seemed that Lottie's host had a permanent need to be somewhere better. From daily walks along the avenue or through the cathedral grounds to visits with her peers—something which Lottie found tiresome, as all they did was tittle-tattle and scandal-monger—and the two of them dined twice weekly at Sir Holden's small estate, a short carriage ride away.

Sir Holden's carriage, which he put at their disposal, transported them to and from the gentleman's residence, for Lady Anne had sent Holmes back to Ringwood. There was insufficient room to house a fourth in her apartment, and Maggie, acting as ladies' maid to both women, slept on a trundle at the foot of Lottie's bed. Even as a servant in Lady Eleanor's household, each had their own room. Lottie was sorry for Maggie's discomfort, as she heard her toss and turn throughout the night.

Lottie felt warmly toward Sir Holden, who was thoughtful and respectful, dividing his attention equally between the two of them. Although Lottie was aware of his lingering gazes towards her, his soft eyes becoming more adoring with each visit. Lady Anne, on the other hand, looked at Lottie with narrowed eyes, as if she disapproved of the gentleman's affection for her ward, yet she continued to accept his invitations.

Her thoughts were broken by a woman's voice hushing an excited group of children, and Lottie recognised the governess charged with Freya's three girls.

"Good afternoon, Miss Colton," the governess nodded her head, accompanied by a pink-cheeked smile. "The young ladies spotted you from a distance, and we made haste to catch you."

The three girls curtsied beautifully to Lottie and Lady Anne, and a fourth girl, close in age to the oldest of Freya's daughters, smiled shyly and bobbed in greeting.

"I am very pleased to see you all, and so unexpectedly." Lottie was delighted to have a diversion from Lady Anne if she were honest. "Are you finished with your studies already?"

The two youngest girls took one of Lottie's hands in theirs, and the oldest girl, Marie, linked arms with the other girl, who looked vaguely familiar. Lottie looked to Lady Anne, who she knew was not overly fond of children, never having had any of her own, who sniffed and waved her fan dismissively. The girls tugged Lottie back to their picnic blanket a short distance away, where a delicate toy tea party was laid out.

Freya's daughters, Marie, Michaela, and Missy, fussed over Lottie and their friend, pouring them lukewarm tea from the child-sized china teapot into tiny cups with matching saucers.

"Miss Arya, how do you take your tea?" Marie asked her friend, and the girls dissolved into giggles.

The moment the fourth little girl smiled, Lottie recognised her, the girl from the park in London, Lord Audley-Sinclair and Amelia's secret child.

Lottie glanced over to see how Lady Anne was occupied and saw her approach a gentleman, Sir Anthony Shepherd, who stood a short distance away next to the Royal bandstand. Lady Anne curtsied to the gentleman and his companion, a lady who was already acquainted with Lottie's chaperone.

Sir Shepherd cast a wide glance around, no doubt expecting to see Lottie nearby, but she ducked her head, taking a sip of the cold tea, rather than be seen by the lecherous gentleman.

After some minutes, Arya was as relaxed as the Antcliffe girls and Lottie passed the time playing with the children. Their game of chase became a little noisy, and Lottie saw Lady Anne and her group heading toward them. The governess was already packing up their picnic and had signalled to a coachman who lingered nearby to collect the hamper.

"Come now, girls. It's high time we returned to Freshford," the governess called as she attempted to herd the girls.

"What fun you have been having," Lady Anne trilled from a short distance, and all activity stopped.

Lottie felt a small hand slide into hers, and she glanced down to see Arya.

"May I present my ward, Miss Amelia Colton. Amelia, this is my very good friend, Marchioness DeWinter, and, of course, you and Sir Shepherd are already acquainted. And the Misses Antcliffe and—" Lady Anne's voice trailed off as greetings were exchanged.

The Marchioness was a delightful lady; however, Lottie disliked the way Sir Shepherd constantly shifted his eyes from her to Arya and back, with an almost greedy grin on his red shiny face. She felt increasingly uncomfortable and was immensely glad when the governess gathered the girls and left.

The remaining foursome began to move, with Lady Anne and the Marchioness strolling sedately in front. Lottie clasped her hands behind her back and tried to avoid the stumbling gait of Sir Shepherd, which brought them into regular contact.

"Pretty little thing," Sir Shepherd mumbled the next time he came close, too close.

Lady Anne glanced over her shoulder, and Lottie was sure she saw her nod in satisfaction. If her ward had this gentleman in mind for a suitor, Lottie vowed to make her objections—and there were many—known.

As they parted ways, Sir Shepherd pressed a sloppy kiss to the back of Lottie's hand, leaving a mark on her white glove. Once she and Lady Anne returned to the apartment, Lottie made sure to scrub the offending article with lye and hot water in order to rid herself of the tainted feeling being around that man gave her.

***

Over the ensuing weeks, Lady Anne, it seemed to Lottie, went out of her way to orchestrate an invitation to all the same gatherings as Sir Shepherd, from dinner at the Marchioness' grand house to an impromptu masked ball at the assembly rooms. At every turn, Lottie found herself in far too close contact with the man who made her skin crawl and who himself was making his designs on Lottie quite clear.

At a masked ball in early July, Lottie wore a mask, but not one with a wooden dowel to hold in the hand. She had Maggie replace the dowel with ribbon so that she could tie it tightly to her head and keep her identity hidden for longer. She took up position behind a tall potted fern so that she could observe the room and its occupants. As much as she was keen to avoid Sir Shepherd, she also looked out for Lord Audley-Sinclair, who one might expect to attend at least one event in Bath during the time she was there. She could gladly endure an entire evening pinned to that particular gentleman's side rather than a single dance with the ever slimier and more suspicious Sir Shepherd.

"My dear Amelia." Lottie heard a woman's voice call softly, and she parted the branches of a tall plant behind which she was hiding. "I will protect you from whomever you are hiding."

Lottie's thoughts immediately went to Lord Audley-Sinclair, and she felt his absence as she moved to stand next to Freya, who lowered her mask with a smile.

"I am so very pleased to see you, your Grace." Lottie curtsied, and Freya took her hand.

"We have been apart far too long. The girls enjoyed their time with you at the Royal Crescent; they are very fond of you, as am I. You will stay with us before you return to Ringwood Manor."

"I would like that very well, your Grace," Lottie nodded. "I do not wish to take you away from the company you already have at Freshford."

Freya looked at her in question.

"Miss Arya's parents?" Lottie saw a flash of something cross the duchess' face before her composure returned.

"Little Arya is the ward of a very, very important man in society, my dear. The gentleman asked me to take care of Arya for the duration of the summer, while his business takes him overseas." Freya looked around to ensure they were alone. "I tell you this in the strictest of confidence, Amelia. The gentleman has reason to believe there is a genuine threat to Arya's safety, and he entrusted her to my care, to keep her out of harm's way."

At that point, Freya was called away, and Lottie was left alone with her thoughts. The gentleman calling himself Arya's guardian was surely Lord Audley-Sinclair, although Lottie knew differently, that he was actually the girl's father. It would explain his absence from the social calendar if he was away on business.

Slightly more at ease now she had a visit to Freshford to look forward to, Lottie left her hiding place and began to mingle. Sir Shepherd was last seen disappearing to an anteroom with a bottle of something under his arm and an older woman under the other, so Lady Anne informed her, and Lottie accepted several offers to dance, finally enjoying herself.

Many dances later, Lottie took refreshment and visited the powder room, where she adjusted her mask. As she left, she realised she had not fastened the ribbons holding her mask sufficiently, and she lifted both hands to retie it.

"Such a pretty little thing," a man slurred from behind her, and two hands grasped Lottie around the middle, far too far above her waist to be decent.

Lottie turned, her mask falling to the floor, and tried to push a very drunken Sir Shepherd away. His wet, mobile lips spread in a grin, exposing his less than white teeth. But his hold was too strong.

"No need to hide your beauty behind a mask, Amelia. Come, let me hold you like I used to."

He started to pull her towards him, and Lottie pressed her hands against his chest, pushing with all her might.

"Ha ha, I always liked our little games of rough and tumble before—" He slid his tongue across his lower lip and scoffed suggestively.

"Sir, unhand me this instant, I implore you," Lottie gasped, as Sir Shepherd wrapped one arm around her waist, and she felt his round middle pressing against her.

Lottie looked around for assistance, but there was nobody to come to her aid. The ball was in full swing, and Sir Shepherd was fully in his cups.

"Our time apart has made you frosty, my girl. Let my hands warm you, let my mouth—" The man growled and pressed one hand to Lottie's bosom, squeezing firmly.

Lottie shivered in revulsion, her cheeks coloured with humiliation, but she swung her hand toward his face. The sharp slap did not leave so much as an imprint on his alcohol-reddened cheek, but it did stop his very unwelcome advances.

"Why do you fight me, when we both know that you're not the good girl you claim to be, Amelia?" He laughed excessively loudly and wobbled back and forth on unsteady legs. "I recall the nights you waited for me to return, laid ready and waiting flat on your back, your legs spread."

Lottie, raised by a lady of the night, was not unaware of the mechanics of intimacy, but to hear this supposed gentleman slurring Amelia's memory was shocking beyond belief.

"If I remember rightly, you were particularly fond of being taken from—"

"That is enough, sir." Another man's voice filled Lottie's ears, and for a split second, she thought, nay hoped, it was Lord Audley-Sinclair come to her rescue.

Sir Anthony Holden bodily removed Sir Shepherd to a nearby anteroom before returning to a shaken Lottie, and gently led her to the cloakroom.

"Fetch Lady Anne Gilroy, boy, make it snappy," Sir Anthony bid a servant, before turning to Lottie. "Madam, I apologise unreservedly for that man's undignified and loutish behaviour. Most unbecoming of a gentleman, and I am horrified at what you endured."

"Thank you, Sir Anthony," Lottie demurred, dazed at how quickly the course of the evening changed. "I beg of you, please do not trouble my Lady Anne with the events. She thinks very highly of the gentleman concerned, and I do not wish to upset her unnecessarily."

"Of course, my dear." Sir Anthony bowed, just as Lady Anne bustled into the cloakroom, looking mightily annoyed at being diverted from her conversation with her friends.

"What is wrong, child?" The older woman snapped, and Sir Anthony bristled protectively, moving closer to Lottie.

"Madam, your ward is quite overwhelmed and should retire for the evening. I will make your apologies to our host on your behalf." He bowed and cast a soft gaze toward Lottie. "I will call upon you tomorrow afternoon, Lady Anne, if I may?"

"You are most welcome, sir." She curtsied, her smile pleasant, but as soon as Sir Anthony had left, she turned to Lottie with a sneer. "What trouble have you gotten yourself into now, my girl?"

Chapter 14

The following afternoon, when Maggie announced the arrival of Sir Anthony Holden to Lady Anne, Lottie was summarily dismissed to her room.

"Miss Colton has taken to her bed with a summer chill, Sir Holden." Lady Anne's shrill tone floated through the apartment. "She has asked me to relay her sincere apologies for the inconvenience."

"I am sorely saddened to hear this, my Lady," Sir Anthony responded, and the rest of the conversation was hushed as they went out to the balcony, one of the most redeeming features of the apartment.

Lottie sat upon her bed, waiting for her release, and all too soon, Lady Anne threw open the door to the bedroom.

"He has gone, but not before telling me a little of what went on last evening."

Lottie stood so as not to have Lady Anne towering over her. There was already sufficient disapproval and judgement emanating from every pore of the woman's body.

"And what did Sir Anthony recount?"

"Suffice it to say, the retelling of events was censored and discreet. What were you thinking, allowing yourself to be alone with Sir Shepherd?"

"He forced himself upon me, my Lady, I did not encourage nor welcome his advances. The man is abhorrent to me." Lottie felt the unspoken blame landing heavily on her shoulders. "I went to the powder room, and he was there."

Lottie's body shivered at the memory, and she wrapped her arms around her middle for comfort. That was one thing she knew would not be forthcoming from Lady Anne.

Lady Anne narrowed her eyes for a moment.

"Duchess Antcliffe informed me that she had asked you to stay at Freshford, should you be amenable to the invitation?"

Lottie's spirits lifted, and her opinion wavered. Perhaps this was her chaperone's attempt at compassion, and for that, she was grateful.

"I should indeed, my Lady, if you can do without me for the duration of my stay." Lottie curtsied rather than hug the woman like she would have done if it were Maggie before her.

"Quite." Lady Anne sniffed. "I made do without you for many a year, child, I dare say I can manage without you for a few days."

***

Freya greeted Lottie with open arms the moment she entered the high-ceilinged hallway at Freshford two days later.

"Amelia, welcome."

"I am truly glad to be here, your Grace." Lottie managed a curtsy, but Freya pulled her up.

"No, no, none of that. We are friends, Amelia, you will call me Freya. Come."

Freya linked her arm and guided her to a small sitting room, Freya's private space, where Lottie had not yet been invited.

"I am desperate to talk to you. I almost sent for you yesterday, so anxious was I for your arrival."

"Your Gr—, Freya, what ever is wrong?"

Freya's hands twisted one over the other, and Lottie could see her friend was disturbed.

"His Grace is away on a hunting trip in the North; otherwise I am sure such a thing would never have occurred."

Lottie slid to the edge of her seat.

"Start from the beginning," she said.

Freya gave a grateful look and nodded.

"Last night, the staff caught an intruder trying to break into the house. They saw him off, but he had attempted to make entry to the nursery, smashing the window. The girls were frightened half to death."

"How awful."

"Both governesses, ours and Arya's, have reported a man lurking when they have been on outings, and on one occasion, he tried to lure Arya away from my girls. It doesn't bear thinking about what his true intentions were."

Freya's eyes filled with tears.

"You must not blame yourself, Freya. These incidents are beyond your control, you must see that." Lottie slipped from her seat and knelt on the floor in front of Freya, taking her hands in hers.

"But I do, I do." Freya's voice rose in anguish. "The Lord entrusted me with Arya's care, with her safety, and I have failed on numerous occasions."

Freya did not register that she had identified Arya's ward as a Lord, whereas before she had called him a gentleman. Lottie firmly believed she was the only one who knew the true identity of Arya's parents because Lord Audley-Sinclair identified himself only as her guardian. He was actively denying his true connection to the child.

If the Lord was willing to risk Arya's safety by handing his daughter's care to another—and Lottie did not apportion any blame to Freya in this matter—Lottie felt it was down to her to take action to protect Amelia's precious child. She owed it to Amelia and Lady Eleanor's memories to keep the girl safe.

Freya, having shared her burden with Lottie, was calmer, and they talked more generally about what they planned to do with the girls during Lottie's stay, to keep them close and keep their minds off the attempted break-in.

Lottie, as she lay in her four-poster bed that night, pondered why someone would want to take Arya, what they hoped to gain. But she was sure that it was related to Nathaniel and his nefarious dealings. Strangers in dark corners could not make trustworthy bedfellows, and who knew how many enemies the man's unnamed profession would garner.

As the only person in full possession of the facts, it was down to her, in Nathaniel's absence, to protect his daughter from this stranger.

***

Later that afternoon, once the girls had finished their studies, the thunder of feet alerted Lottie to the imminent arrival of three very excited little girls. Only Arya hung back as her friends greeted Lottie effusively. Once Marie, Michaela, and Missy had told her all their news, they followed the bell calling them to afternoon tea. Lottie stood from her chair where she had been reading in the library while Freya saw to some household business and held out her hand to the little girl.

Arya smiled shyly and reached out. Holding her hot little hand stirred something deep inside Lottie. She had never experienced such a simple gesture as holding hands with her mother as a child because her mother was busy holding many other things in hers. Lottie knew in that moment, without a single doubt, that she would do whatever it took to look after Arya until such a time Nathaniel returned.

From that point forward, Arya became Lottie's little shadow, which Freya thought was very sweet. When the time came for Lottie to return to Lady Anne's apartment before heading home for Ringwood Manor, Arya became desolate and pleaded for Miss Amelia to stay.

Freya sent word to Lady Anne that due to the duke's continued absence, she would very much like Amelia to stay on as companion to her and the girls, and would Lady Anne be particularly upset if she were to purloin her ward for another week.

Lady Anne, under normal circumstances, would be extremely put out. However, it came to light, in the hastily written note that Maggie secretly sent to Lottie via the manservant along with Lady Anne's reply, that the Lady was often absent most evenings, dining with Sir Anthony, visiting the theatre, or attending events as his guest. Maggie was enjoying the freedom and told Lottie she could spend as long as she liked with the duchess at Freshford because she was extremely comfortable sleeping in Lottie's bed.

Over dinner that evening, Lottie enquired of Freya when she expected the duke to return from his hunting trip.

"I suspect Arya's guardian will make a return to Bath before my husband finds his way home." Freya waved her fork about as she spoke, pausing to take a bite of the delicious haunch of venison. "I am lucky the duke does not have any philandering ways about him, unlike other gentlemen known to us both."

Lottie wanted to ask if Freya was talking about Nathaniel, but the conversation moved on.

When Lottie retired to her bedroom for the evening, she found Arya curled up in her bed, and although she should have woken her or carried her back to her own bedroom in the nursery, she did not have the heart. The child, so innocent and even more so in repose, was certainly the most precious thing, and Lottie wondered what would happen if she were to take Arya back to Ringwood Manor with her. It would be to keep her safe until Nathaniel returned, until she could make her feelings clear on the subject.

She imagined telling him that he needed to do his duty as Arya's father. The child should feel safe, loved, and wanted, not hidden away in the city, nor shipped from place to place, stranger to stranger, entrusting her care to someone else.

Lottie would never do that if she had the privilege of having a child, and until Arya's father returned, she would step into the maternal role without hesitation. If that meant sharing a bed with Arya, then so be it.

***

The duke returned a few days later, and to celebrate his homecoming, Freya organised an impromptu gathering, inviting their friends, acquaintances, and the important people in Bath and the surrounding areas. The girls were very excited at the prospect of being allowed to stay up for the first hour or so of the party, primped and preened as seriously as any Lady preparing for her evening.

Arya was a little unsure, as she watched Lottie get ready, helping her on with her dress and fastening buttons.

"What happens at a party?" Arya asked.

"Lots of things," Lottie explained. "The women gossip and dance and refuse to eat anything for fear of appearing greedy. The gentlemen eat and drink, talk about the war, and occasionally dance."

"Who will you dance with?" Arya stood before the mirror, held out her skirts, and practiced the dance steps Lottie had taught her and the girls that afternoon.

Lottie smiled indulgently as she watched the little girl. She definitely would avoid any contact with Sir Shepherd and would certainly not dance with him. She would indulge Sir Holden if he should ask to say thank you for coming to her rescue at the last ball.

"I will dance with you, Arya," Lottie said laughingly as she came to stand behind the girl and hugged her close.

Arya's face glowed, and her smile was as wide as Lottie had ever seen. What a difference in the child, when she felt like she belonged to somebody, belonged somewhere. If Lottie could do anything to keep the girl feeling that way, she would.

***

When the governesses came to collect their young charges, the girls protested, but they were happily tired and, Lottie thought, secretly glad to go to bed.

"I promise to come and check on you a little later." Lottie bent to kiss Arya goodnight.

"What if I'm asleep?" Arya yawned and hugged Lottie.

Lottie wanted nothing more than to lift Arya into her arms and take her to bed herself, as she usually did.

"I'll leave a flower on your pillow, so when you wake, you'll know I was there."

***

After dancing continuously for an hour, Lottie slipped from the ballroom to fulfil her promise to Arya. On the way, she took a rose from one of the many floral displays and slipped up the backstairs, which she knew was the quickest way to the nursery. It was a habit ingrained from her days as a maid for Lady Eleanor, and the Freshford servants were used to seeing the young lady.

As Lottie approached the nursery, she could see a shadowy figure in the doorway, and her steps slowed. The figure, a man, was well dressed, precluding him from being a servant, so he must be a guest from the party. The figure stepped back into the hallway, closing the nursery door, and Lottie recognised the uneven gait of a man in his cups.

Sir Anthony Shepherd.

"Sir, are you lost?" Lottie called out, drawing the man's attention as she walked towards him. "These are private quarters; you must have taken a wrong turn."

The man lurched toward her, an evil glint in his eyes.

"You're the duchess' little pet, now, Amelia, are you?"

"Sir Shepherd, there are many young ladies desperate for your attention in the ballroom." Lottie had his measure after their last encounter.

The man—no gentleman—was a lech and believed he was still a catch. Lottie believed he had acted the same toward Amelia years before, which was why he had made those lewd comments. He must have her confused with some other woman he had been intimate with because Amelia would not have given him the time of day.

Besides, her letters spoke of a handsome man who made her feel wanted and loved. She cared for that man sufficiently to be intimate, to create a life with, and Sir Shepherd would never even slightly resemble someone of that calibre.

"Are you desperate, Amelia? You were always so desperate for someone to love you."

Lottie was disgusted by the sour breath that came in her direction as he spoke, and she ensured she kept just out of his reach as she drew him back towards the main stairs.

"Not I, sir, but I am sure you will find a willing partner in the ballroom."

He followed her down the first flight of stairs, stumbling slightly, but he caught himself on the curved banister.

"You are different from before," he slurred, and Lottie assumed he was talking about the weeks previous when he groped her.

"My hair is a little different, perhaps." She humoured him as they descended, and once they were in the ballroom, she decided it was time to execute a plan to remove Arya from this danger.

"Your hair, your eyes, the way you speak, the way you move." Sir Shepherd seemed to gain some clarity, and his unfocused gaze seemed to sharpen as soon as they reached the doorway to the ballroom. "You are a completely different person than the Amelia Colton I knew so well. She was soft, but you, you are harder, colder."

"You are inebriated, Sir Anthony," Lottie said warily. "Be careful with your words, or I may be forced to share what I know of you. That you have attempted on several occasions to abduct a child."

"What you know of me?" Sir Shepherd laughed heartily as the servants opened the double doors.

The master of ceremonies opened his mouth to announce the return of Sir Anthony Shepherd and Miss Amelia Colton. Lottie was horrified at the prospect of being linked in any way with this man and tried to drop back.

But the man grabbed her arm roughly and pulled her into the room as they were announced.

"Attention, all." Sir Shepherd's loud voice carried to the farthest corner of the room, and even the musicians paused their playing.

"Sir Anthony, please," Lottie begged under her breath.

"You have been introduced to this young woman, who claims to be Miss Amelia Colton. I can reveal that she is an imposter. The real Amelia, the love of my life, passed away some years ago, a heartbreaking truth I have kept to myself to protect Amelia's family."

He thrust Lottie onto the quickly emptying dance floor so that she could be seen by everyone gathered, Lady Anne, Freya, the duke, the Misses Hayes, and even Sir James Holden.

"This chit of a girl is a fraud."

Chapter 15

Nathaniel was exhausted from his long trip back from Cadiz and could have waited until the next morning to go to Freshford to collect Arya. But he found out there was a ball that evening, and if he rode hard enough, he would catch the tail end of it.

Not only was he keen to know that Arya was safe and sound, for he had asked the duchess not to communicate with him in any shape or form during his absence, but he had missed the social niceties of England. A ball was enough to lift any weary traveller's spirits, with good wine and good company.

Also in his thoughts was Miss Amelia Colton. He looked forward to knowing if Lady Anne had kept her end of their bargain while he was away, preventing any engagement or association of the young lady with either Sir Holden or Sir Shepherd.

On the way up the long driveway at Freshford leading to the house, Nathaniel passed many carriages, and he wondered if he was later than he thought, if the guests were leaving already. The duke and duchess were known for their generosity and bonhomie at their gatherings, which often did not finish until the early hours of the morning.

"Lord Nathaniel Audley-Sinclair," the Master of Ceremonies announced to an all but empty ballroom.

The musicians were packing away their instruments, and the servants were clearing tables of plates piled high with food and collecting glasses that were nearly full. Nathaniel wondered what had happened to drive the people away.

The duchess, being comforted by the duke, looked at Nathaniel with tear-filled eyes as he approached.

"Your Graces," Nathaniel murmured as he bowed deeply, feeling ill at ease with the situation.

"My Lord," Freya greeted him, but her voice broke and the tears spilled onto her cheeks. "How will you ever forgive me?"

Nathaniel looked from the duchess to the duke, extremely puzzled, and waited with barely concealed impatience as the duke signalled for one of his wife's friends to take her away.

"Nathaniel." The duke placed a heavy hand on Nathaniel's shoulder and drew him out through the French doors to the terrace.

A servant closed the doors behind him, and the duke took a hip flask from his pantaloons and took a swig. He held it out to Nathaniel, who was still nonplussed, and it would have been discourteous to refuse.

"This is a terrible to do, and I can only offer my most sincere apologies for the situation in which we find ourselves."

"Indeed, your Grace," Nathaniel nodded. "Might you enlighten me on this matter, sir?"

The duke took another swig, fastened the top, and tucked it back in his pocket.

"Miss Amelia Colton has been my wife's guest at Freshford for the past ten days. During that time, Arya and she have formed a close bond. In addition, I have been made aware that during my absence—hunting in Northumberland, you see—an individual has made several attempts to get close to young Arya, and it appears, that Miss, er—" The duke cleared his throat. "Miss Colton accused Sir Anthony Shepherd of being that individual, having found him loitering in the doorway of our nursery. Where our children and young Arya slept."

"Where is Miss Colton now, sir?" Nathaniel turned to go back into the house, but the duke's next words stopped him in his tracks.

"Gone."

"Gone where, your Grace?"

"It is not known; I am sorry to say. I have dispatched my men to Bath, to Lady Anne's apartment and nearby establishments."

The way the older man lowered his head did not bode well, and Nathaniel was sure he had not heard the whole story.

"Why so much concern for this girl?" Nathaniel asked, even though he was starting to suspect that what he knew about her was now common knowledge.

What else could clear a ballroom so suddenly? A horrible thought occurred to Nathaniel that the girl had left with someone. Surely not Shepherd? He was loathe to ask.

"With whom did the girl leave, your Grace?"

"Arya. She took Arya, Nathaniel, but not before being humiliated by Sir Shepherd. He exposed her masquerade in front of everyone here. She has, apparently, fooled us all. The girl is not Amelia Colton."

Nathaniel started to pace along the terrace, his hands clasping and unclasping at his sides. This made absolutely no sense. Not the part about Amelia's unmasking; that was inevitable. He was mildly surprised it had taken so long. The girl did not strike him as dangerous, despite the risks she had taken in supposing another's identity.

Knowing that Shepherd, Arya's father, had been the individual that Amelia identified as showing too much interest in the child was far more alarming than knowing Arya was with Amelia, or whatever the girl's real name was.

Nathaniel had kept Arya tucked away for good reason. He had promised Amelia—the real Amelia—that he would keep her daughter safe. There was no way on this earth that he would not keep that promise.

"I feel completely responsible, Nathaniel, and I know Freya will never forgive herself. You entrusted that child's very life to us. And now—"

The duke's shoulders fell, and he looked suddenly old. He was seven years older than Nathaniel, but he was reminded of the older conscripts under his command in the latter years of the Napoleonic wars. Their bones were tired, their spirits broken. Yet Duke Antcliffe had never seen battle. He had been pensioned from the cavalry on medical grounds without leaving England.

"I cannot apportion any blame for other's actions to your or your wife, your Grace. Please do not trouble yourself. I will take care of this matter." Nathaniel's response was calm, demonstrating his control.

The strength in Nathaniel's voice gave courage to the duke, and he stood straighter, his voice stronger.

"Indeed. You will, of course, let me know if you need any assistance. Any at all."

Nathaniel bowed deeply and re-entered the house, stalking across the dance floor and into the grand hallway. He glanced up the curved staircase and saw three concerned little faces watching him through the banisters.

Two women appeared on the landing. One he recognised as Arya's governess who headed down toward him as the other guided the three little girls back up the stairs.

"My Lord." The woman's voice was full of emotion, as she curtsied to her master. "The children were safely tucked up in bed and fast asleep when I retired for the evening."

"Mrs. O'Hara, I have known you my entire life, and I trust you implicitly. This is not your fault."

Nathaniel took both the woman's shaking hands in his.

"You will find our girl, will you not, sir?"

"I will, indeed." He nodded, wishing he felt so certain inside. "Rest this evening, Mrs. O'Hara, and travel back to the Windsor house, so that you can be ready when I bring Arya home."

***

Availing himself of a fresh horse from the Freshford stables, Nathaniel rode hard for the centre of Bath to the apartment of Lady Anne. He did not think highly of the woman, but if there was anyone who could give him the information he desperately needed, it was she.

Locating the apartment, he hammered on the door, and it took a while for someone to answer. A short, round-faced woman with a shock of white curls, who was definitely not Lady Anne, answered the door with a soft Northern burr.

"My Lord, how may I be of service?" She bobbed slightly in curtsy.

"I must speak to Lady Anne immediately, madam."

Nathaniel knew the woman was a servant, he remembered her from Ringwood Manor, but he still gave respect to his elders.

"Please come in. I will awaken my lady from her slumber at once."

He strode up and down the surprisingly small parlour as he waited, and in time, a pale version of Lady Anne entered the room.

"My dear Lady Anne." Nathaniel bowed deeply and crossed to her to kiss her outstretched hand. "I beg your pardon for the late hour, but you are the only person I believe who can tell me what I need to know."

Nathaniel saw the woman who answered the door drop her gaze as he sought it, and if Lady Anne would not help, he had a feeling that the maid knew the full story.

"Pray tell, Lord Audley-Sinclair." Lady Anne took a seat and gave him a condescending gaze.

"Your ward, Miss Amelia Colton. It has been revealed this is not her true identity."

Lady Anne merely nodded rather than voice agreement.

"Who is she truly, Lady Anne? She has absconded with my ward, Arya, a six-year-old girl. I am beside myself with worry for her safety."

She wrinkled her nose in distaste as if the whole matter was beneath her.

"The girl was maid to my late sister-in-law, Lady Eleanor Gilroy, for five years, my Lord. Lady Eleanor, in her last hours, as we gathered at her bedside, mistook the girl for her absent niece, Miss Amelia Colton. The solicitor present compounded the mistake and assumed the girl was the sole heir to the Ringwood estate."

Nathaniel's fingernails dug into his palms as he balled his hands into tight fists. The girl he had kissed in the back alleys of Holborn was a mere servant. Never in this life had he made advances to anyone in service. He had not been fooled by her assumed identity, but he had not imagined this.

"I am assuming she is not here?" Nathaniel asked directly to the servant, although both women present shook their heads. "Has she returned to Ringwood?"

"I know not of the girl's intentions, my Lord," Lady Anne said, sounding not even the least regretful. "I had an agreement with her to present her to society, to assist her in making a suitable match. Of course, that was superseded by my subsequent agreement with yourself to prevent a match with Sir Holden and Sir Shepherd."

"Is there anything else I need to know, my Lady, any connections I should be aware of? Anyone else who may have influence over her?"

"I know of none, sir."

Nathaniel, frustrated, bowed once more and headed for the exit. The maid waited with a hand on the door fastening.

"Madam, you know this girl. I have two questions only."

She nodded.

"Will she take care of my girl, Arya?" His voice cracked at the mention of her name, and the maid reached out to touch his arm in reassurance.

"*My girl* will take care of Arya like she was her own."

Nathaniel was of the same opinion but was reassured to hear it from someone who knew her well.

"What do you call your girl?" Nathaniel dropped his voice, his heart beating a little quicker with anticipation.

He had waited many months, since the afternoon of Lady Eleanor's funeral, for the answer. Amelia had never fitted her quite well enough, like a borrowed item of clothing that was a little too tight or a little too short.

"Charlotte Green, my Lord."

The maid curtsied as she opened the door, and Nathaniel stepped out, armed with the knowledge that his future, Arya's future, lay in the hands of a girl called Charlotte.

Chapter 16

"Miss Amelia." Arya's voice sounded so young, so thin in the depths of the night air.

Lottie looked down at the girl, whose eyes were large and shadowed in her face.

"You must call me Miss Lottie, remember, my love," Lottie told her, giving her hand a squeeze. "I am your governess; you are my pupil."

"Miss Lottie, my feet hurt."

Lottie, with her masquerade over and any reputation in tatters, had travelled to Ringwood with Arya over the course of a week. They zigzagged across the southwest of England, never moving in a straight line. As much as she wanted to be home, she knew that Holmes had shut down the whole household while Lottie and Maggie were in Bath, and he had travelled to visit his brother and family for a few weeks. He was not due back for a week after Lottie left Bath.

Her plan, as such, was only to stay in Ringwood as long as it took to recover and gather what she needed. It would not be safe to stay there for any length of time. Ringwood Manor would be an obvious choice for any of the men that the duke or Nathaniel sent after her.

Lottie shifted the small pack she had tied to her back, moving it to the front of her body, and told Arya to climb up. She was sure there was only another mile or so to go until they reached home; she would carry this darling girl for as many miles and as long as it took until they were safe.

Another hour later, Lottie slipped through the rusty gate behind the stables and crunched across the gravel driveway to the front door. She was unsure how many of the household were back from their break, and she could see no lights on at all. Taking a deep breath, she lifted the heavy knocker and let it fall against the brass plate. The sound echoed loudly, and Lottie gently adjusted the sleeping Arya on her back, careful not to wake her.

She waited for what felt like a lifetime until she heard the bolts being drawn back, one by one. When the door opened and she saw a sleepy Holmes holding a candle, her breath rushed from her, followed by a sob of relief.

"Come in, my girl, you are home."

Holmes shut the door behind them and relieved Lottie of the sleeping child. Once Arya was tucked up on the chaise, wrapped in a warm blanket, Lottie allowed herself to fall into the loving embrace of the only father figure she had ever known.

"What have I done, Mr. Holmes?"

His hold tightened momentarily at the vulnerability in her voice, and he held her at arm's length so he could look at her closely.

"I have no doubt you have made the right decision in the moment, Lottie. Life is just a series of choices, and if your heart is true, good will win out in the end." Holmes pressed a kiss to her forehead. "The journey is not always smooth, as you have already discovered, but anything of value is worth the trouble."

Tears trickled down Lottie's cheeks, streaking the dirt, so exhausted was she.

"Get a good night's sleep, Lottie, let your body rest, and everything will look brighter on the morrow."

Nodding, Lottie moved to pick up Arya, but Holmes stilled her hands, lifting the little girl with ease. Numbly, Lottie followed Holmes up the stairs and automatically turned toward the smaller staircase that would lead them up to her attic room, but Holmes turned toward the guest suite.

"This house is yours, Lottie, no matter what has happened. You no longer sleep in the attic."

Too tired to deny it, Lottie tucked Arya into bed and fell asleep as soon as she lay her head on the pillow.

***

Awakening early, leaving the child to sleep, Lottie went down to the kitchen to light the fire, put a kettle of water on to boil, and make a small pan of porridge. Holmes joined her for breakfast.

"Arya is the true heir to Ringwood Manor, Mr. Holmes," Lottie told him.

His brows lifted in surprise.

"How did you come to know this?"

Lottie blushed as she explained how she had found Miss Amelia's letters to Lady Eleanor. While Holmes and Maggie had gone along with the pretence, Lottie had never admitted the full truth to anyone.

"You must think very ill of me, sir." Lottie hung her head, as the full weight of her actions weighed heavy.

"No, child. I brought you to Ringwood Manor, to Lady Eleanor, to keep you safe. How is what you are doing any different?" Holmes rested his hand over Lottie's. "Was Arya in danger?"

"Yes, yes."

"Then my thoughts and feelings for you, Lottie dear, have not changed, nor will they. But, if that danger is following you, it is unwise for you to stay here."

Lottie stood, collected the breakfast dishes, and placed them in the sink.

"We will go to London, to Cheapside, where I grew up. Nobody, aside from you and Maggie, knows where I come from, just as nobody missed me when I ran away from that life."

Returning to the table, Lottie grasped the back of the chair.

"I can pass myself as Arya's governess, or she can be my younger sister, or even my daughter."

"And what will you do for money? I would willingly give you what savings Maggie and I have. There is Lady Eleanor's jewellery sitting untouched in her bedroom."

"No!" Lottie exclaimed loudly and then softened her voice. "I will not touch a penny of Arya's inheritance, Mr. Holmes. Before I knew of her existence, I was willing to take as much as was required until I made a suitable match. Now, the scales have been lifted, the truth, both my own identity and Arya's revealed, and I will admit to my wrongdoing, to the deceit."

"I will never judge you, Lottie," Holmes said, his voice thick with emotion.

He pushed himself out of the chair, its legs scraping across the tiled floor, and he hugged Lottie close like a father would his child.

"We will live as our true selves, as Charlotte Green and Arya Audley-Sinclair." Lottie paused for a moment. "No, Arya Sinclair, as her father's full name will give us away."

***

Later that afternoon, bathed and freshly clothed, their scant belongings packed in two small valises that Holmes found in the attic, Lottie bid goodbye to Ringwood Manor as if she were leaving for the last time.

Arya would become the rightful heir to the manor in due course when she came of age. That was one of the very first things that Lottie would take care of as soon as she had saved enough money to pay for the solicitor. The little girl would be taken care of when she became an adult and would not have to rely on a suitable marriage for her financial security.

Holmes planned to travel to Bath to collect Maggie, to bring her home to the manor. They would continue to keep the house and grounds, until such time Lottie let them know of the stewardship once transferred to Arya and her representative.

But first, he would take Lottie and Arya as far north as Reading, from where he would head west to Bath, and from where they would then take the stage to London.

Arya was excited to return to London, and Lottie had not the heart to squash her dream of returning to her comfortable surroundings in Windsor. She delayed that until they were nearing their final stop, The Swan with Two Necks in Cheapside.

"Arya, we are soon at the end of our journey," Lottie began, and Arya slid across the seat to look out of the window.

Lottie knew that she would not see tall, elegant buildings and green spaces, but narrow streets with houses and businesses crammed together, often on top of each other. This part of London looked and smelled different from what Arya was used to.

"We will be staying here, in Cheapside."

"Where will we live?" Arya asked, her expression curious, rather than fearful or worried.

"I cannot answer that, my love, not yet." Lottie smiled.

"We are on another adventure, Miss Lottie." The girl giggled and returned her attention to the view outside.

Dusk was falling, and the gas lighters could be seen lighting the lamps as the stall-holders started to pack up their wares. Alighting at the large coaching inn, Arya's eyes widened at the hustle and bustle of the courtyard, where a number of coaches had recently arrived and were about to depart.

Lottie knew they should leave as soon as possible, in case they were recognised, which was also why she would not look for work in such a busy hostelry on the main road. She would choose a smaller inn, deep in the back streets to lessen the chance of their discovery.

"Are you ready, Arya?" Lottie picked up both valises, and Arya held her wrist and nodded.

They passed a pair of matronly older women, waiting for their coach, who clucked at Lottie and her young charge.

"You have a beautiful daughter," one said, reaching out to pat Arya's head.

"Thank you, milady." Lottie paused to curtsy her thanks without correcting the woman's assumption, and Arya followed her lead.

The women cooed and waggled their fingers in farewell.

As they walked, Arya's head turning this way and that to take in all the unique sights of Cheapside at night, Lottie tightened her grip on the child's hand.

"The lady thought you were my mother, Miss Lottie," Arya said a little later after they had stopped at two inns while Lottie enquired after work. "My mother died when I was a baby."

Lottie's throat tightened at the matter-of-fact way Arya spoke about Amelia. To date, the child had never mentioned her, or her father, and the variety and ferocity of emotion that swept over Lottie took her by surprise.

Arya had a father, but it was clear that Arya had not been apprised of this knowledge because she would surely have mentioned Nathaniel by now.

"I already have a governess," Arya continued. "Can we make-believe that you are my mother?"

As if Lottie had not already fallen in love with this angelic innocent, her heart swelled with pride at the request.

"Whatever you wish, Arya. I would be honoured."

Lottie stopped walking, put down the valises, and bent to pull the little girl into her arms, holding her tight. As they pulled apart, Arya kissed Lottie's cheek and smiled shyly.

"Mama," she whispered, almost to herself, like she had been waiting to say the word for the longest time.

Lottie had no idea if her own mother was still alive and had no desire to search for her to rekindle that relationship. But she swore to herself that she would be the best mother to this little girl and would love her forever or however long she and Arya were together.

Chapter 17

Getting out of bed, Nathaniel checked his pocket watch by the light of the oil lamp and saw it was not yet even midnight. Exhausted from his journey back from Spain, and his ride from Bath to Winchester, he had supped early at the hotel and fallen into a restless sleep before seven that evening.

Wide awake, Nathaniel dressed rather carelessly, his shirt untucked with no cravat, and made his way down to the bar. The landlord had assured him they would be open until the early hours if he desired ale, company, or a card game.

Nathaniel was welcomed with a flagon of ale, a seat at the card table with the landlord and two other men, and several busty serving girls willing to hang from his shoulders if required.

"Deal me in, sir," Nathaniel instructed as he took a swig of beer and grimaced at the sharpness of the drink.

"You've come from the manor, sir," the landlord said, after several rounds of cards.

"Indeed, my good man," Nathaniel said cheerfully, draining his flagon and signalling for more. "The place was completely deserted, not even a mouse to be seen."

"Holmes, the houseman, is due back later this week." The barmaid supplied the ale and the information.

"Ah yes, I remember the man from the late Lady Eleanor's funeral. Such a sad occasion." Nathaniel nodded. "Left the whole estate to her niece, if I remember."

The locals did not respond, so Nathaniel tried again.

"I was hoping I might have been mentioned in the will, my mother and Lady Eleanor were close friends many years ago. But not to be." He swigged deeply from the cup and pulled out his wallet, unfurling it to reveal the money within. "Let me settle up now, landlord, before I'm in my cups and forget."

"Nay, my Lord. Your word is good enough. Stay a while and allow us a chance to win back what we've lost."

"What else can we bet on, my friends?" Nathaniel waved his arms expansively, letting his gaze land on one of the younger women present. "How about this lovely girl? What say you come and be my wife if I win the next hand?"

The girl smiled awkwardly and moved behind the bar. Nathaniel knew he was stirring the pot, but rich men, especially one with his reputation, were expected to lack morality and manners.

"The girl is not for sale, my Lord."

The landlord brought the conversation back round to Freshford.

"Lady Eleanor's niece left many years ago, sir, if I remember correctly. The girl you refer to was the Lady's maid. The Lady was much confused toward the end," the man explained.

"Ha, lucky girl." Nathaniel laughed.

"In more ways than one, sir," the landlord said. "Holmes, five or six years hence, rescued the girl from being the wager in a card game such as this from a gentleman such as yourself."

"A marriage proposal from a gentleman, a fine wager for a bar wench," Nathaniel guffawed with a wink to the girl behind the bar.

"Lottie was just twelve years old, my Lord." The landlord spread his cards on the table and waited for Nathaniel's move. "Holmes brought the girl to Lady Eleanor, and the Lady took the child into service."

Nathaniel followed suit, without any sleight of hand, and nodded to show the landlord had won.

"You have bettered me, sir," Nathaniel said, deliberately slurring his words.

He pulled several large notes from his wallet, more than enough to cover the bill of everyone in attendance. He was paying not just for the ale, but also for the information.

"Drinks are on me." Nathaniel stood and laid the money on top of the cards. "From maid to mistress of Ringwood Manor, not too shabby a win for a young girl from Winchester."

The landlord stood too, picking up the money and handing it to one of the girls.

"Lottie wasn't from Winchester, sir," he said, smoothing his dirty apron over his round belly. "Story was the girl's mother was a baggage from Cheapside, and Lottie ran away because she wanted more."

Nathaniel pretended to stagger toward the stairs before the man had finished talking, waving his hand in farewell, but he took in the landlord's words carefully. At least he had somewhere to start.

***

Nathaniel knew many shady characters, inevitable in his line of work, who reached out to their network of seedy connections.

After many false starts, the most recent lead finally paid off, and he stood in the shadows watching Lottie sweeping the doorstep of an inn. Her cheeks were pink from exertion, her hair tied back under a headscarf, and her clothes were no longer grand and fancy but plain and utilitarian.

His breath caught in his throat as a small figure exited behind Lottie, showing her a haphazardly folded pile of clothes.

Arya.

She looked the same as when he had last seen her, but different due to her clothing and her location. Arya smiled at whatever Lottie had said, and he heard the child laugh. He had missed that sound in his house, and it was enough to drive him forward.

Arya saw him first, and a smile lit up her face, but it quickly fell as she no doubt recognised his dark frown. She tugged on Lottie's sleeve, and they both looked at him. He was almost upon them, and he was sure they would turn and disappear into the building. But Lottie stood, pushing Arya behind her, and held the broom in both hands as if it were a weapon.

"Lord Audley-Sinclair, good day to you." Lottie's voice was bright and welcoming, and she gave him a curtsy.

"I have nothing to say to you, Miss *Green*." Nathaniel's words were clipped, his eyes barely making contact with her gaze.

The use of the girl's real name caused her cheeks to blanche and her knuckles whitened on the broom, but she did not look away.

Arya peered from under the girl's arm, her eyes wide, and the very sight of her within reach made his voice tight, overly formal.

"You will come with me now, child."

She shook her head, and Lottie's arm shot back to hold Arya tightly against her.

"Do as you are bid this instant." He spoke more loudly than he meant to, and the child squeaked in fear.

"Go inside, my lovely." Lottie's voice was soft, reassuring as she turned to hug the little girl to her with one arm, hanging onto her broom with the other.

Nathaniel stepped forward as Arya disappeared into the darkness of the inn; however, Lottie was immovable and blocked his entrance, only an inch and a broom between the two of them.

"What gives you the right to kidnap the girl and bring her to this place to live in squalor, madam?" His voice was low, menacing, but she did not give way.

"What gives you the right, sir, to hide Arya away, to have other people look after her while you take your leave to who knows where for who knows how long?"

Nathaniel watched the rise of her chest as she took a deep breath as if to continue, but he had plenty to say to her himself.

"Does she know the truth? That you are nothing but a servant?" Leaning over her, he spat the last word with disdain, the invisible taste of their location sour in his mouth.

He meant to intimidate her, but she lifted her chin so she could look him directly in the eye.

"Aye, she does, my Lord. Arya knows everything about me, servant and all. She asks, and I tell. Can you say the same?"

"The girl has no need to know about my affairs. What else have you exposed her to, in this filthy tavern, with its drunks and its whores? You have shaded her propriety before she has any need for any."

"You call her girl, sir. I call her Arya, my love, my angel. I show her I love her so that she knows she is loved, no matter what else I might be lacking." Lottie pushed against Nathaniel with the broom, her voice fierce, her eyes shining with tears. "Arya is with me all day; she falls asleep in my arms. I ensure she is not exposed to any impropriety. Quite the opposite, I surround her with good honest people who care for her, protect her."

Nathaniel was stirred by the passion in Lottie's words, the way her eyes flashed as she spoke.

"You speak of honesty, and yet, you stole the identity, the entitlement of Miss Amelia Colton, a good and decent woman who was taken from this world too soon. What say you, madam, of the deceitful web you wove, ensnaring others in your lies?"

"I did wrong, sir, I admit, and I am determined to make amends for it all. But some things are more important than apologising for my mistakes." Lottie dropped her voice and her eyes for a moment.

"What could be more important than restoring Amelia's good name for propriety's sake?" Nathaniel scoffed, a smug smile tugging at the corner of his mouth, for he had rightly put this maid in her place.

To think he had danced with her on numerous occasions, held her close.

"Arya is more important than anything else, Lord Audley-Sinclair." Lottie thumped her fist against his chest to emphasise her point. "I know you are her father, that you lay with her mother and denied them both for some time, deciding too late that you would honour your responsibilities after Miss Colton passed away."

Nathaniel opened his mouth to deny such a thing, but Lottie was not finished.

"Out of shame, you then hid Arya away, with only a governess for company. Is the encumbrance of such a beautiful child unsuitable for a man of your reputation, sir? Do the ladies whose company you seek preclude the existence of a daughter?"

Lottie took a deep breath, the daring of her words not lost on him, and she exhaled the air from her lungs, her body shuddering with the emotional outburst.

Nathaniel stepped forward, holding Lottie on her feet with one arm around her waist, and brought her through the door with him.

"My Lord," she protested, holding onto the lapels of his coat for balance, dropping her broom. "What do you mean by—"

He did not know what he meant by this, apart from the urgent need to press his lips to hers, silencing her words, and taking her breath, and his, away.

"Miss Green," Nathaniel started, his breathing a little uneven from the feelings that were awoken in him. "I want you to be my wife."

Lottie still had hold of his lapels, her lips damp and parted from his kiss, her eyes round in surprise.

From behind a pillar, Nathaniel heard a gasp and looked around the tavern, realising for the first time that there was an audience other than young Arya. In the silence that followed, only Arya's giggle and clap of hands indicated anyone's excitement.

"For the sake of propriety, sir, I cannot accept," Lottie answered, finally releasing her grip and stepping backwards.

Nathaniel, taken aback by her refusal, might as well have been slapped around the face.

"Arya, you are leaving with me," he blustered, stepping around Lottie as if she did not exist.

He reached for Arya and wrapped his hand around her wrist, expecting her to docilely and willingly oblige.

"No. No, I will not go," Arya shouted, something he had never heard her do before, and chalked another black mark against the serving girl and her bad influence.

Nathaniel tugged on the child's wrist, and she cried out. Lottie, several men who were drinking at the bar, and a barmaid stepped toward him, some with a menacing air. He could have taken any of them on, but was a little out of kilter with the most unexpected of rejections from both Lottie and Arya.

"I will return, Miss Green, to take what is rightly mine," Nathaniel said loudly for all to hear and stalked out of the building.

When he returned, a few hours later, with a signed warrant from Judge Hayes, who he had disturbed defiantly as he drank in his gentlemen's club, and two policemen, he found Lottie and Arya had gone.

"I'll offer ten pounds to any man or woman who will tell me the whereabouts of Miss Green and my ward," Nathaniel called out in the now-packed tavern, waving a banknote in the air.

But no one stirred, nobody spoke, and he had no choice but to leave empty-handed.

Nathaniel had the truth about Lottie now, her upbringing, her intelligence, her nouse, her iron-strong will to do what she believed was right, and the desire to fight for what she wanted. These were all qualities which he would greatly admire in a woman, under different circumstances.

The truth was not as useful as it seemed, however, because he doubted it would be very easy to find them once more. He had overplayed his hand by kissing her, by proposing to her, by mishandling Arya, whom he loved more than anything.

The final truth was that he might never find them again.

Chapter 18

After Nathaniel's marriage proposal, Lottie became even more protective of Arya.

From the moment they packed their meagre belongings back into the valises, Lottie barely let go of Arya's hand. Her eyes looked upon everyone with suspicion. They did not stay anywhere for more than one night, and sometimes only a few hours if a man, or even a woman, paid too much attention to Arya.

It was difficult because, in spite of everything Lottie had put the girl through and exposed her to, Arya's indefatigable spirit, her sense of fun and adventure barely wavered. After several weeks of moving from slum to slum, Lottie was exhausted, on edge, and becoming desperate.

Moving so regularly was expensive, and boarding houses wanted a small deposit, which Lottie invariably forfeited when they left in the middle of the night. Moving out of Cheapside became necessary for cheaper accommodation. But the quality deteriorated the cheaper the hostel.

Arya developed a rash that Lottie was sure came from the stained, damp mattress. Lottie slept sitting up, propped in a corner of the room, with Arya on her lap. She spent the last of her money on a balm from an Indian market stall-holder, who swore it would cure most ills. Lottie was reminded of the doctor that Lady Anne visited, and memories of her time with Lady Eleanor and playing dress up as Amelia left her feeling shamed.

A sensitive child, Arya asked her why she was sad in the middle of the night when the hullabaloo from other inhabitants in the equally tiny rooms kept them awake.

"How can I be sad when I have you?" Lottie forced a smile and pressed a kiss to Arya's forehead.

The rattling of the door handle took both their attentions, and Lottie pressed a finger to Arya's lips, pulling the thin blanket up over their heads. Through a hole in the material, Lottie watched as the door burst open, its flimsy lock broken, and a drunken man wove his way into the room, turning in a circle as if looking for something.

His hand was in the waistband of his long johns, and Lottie covered Arya's eyes so she could not see what the man was about to do. However, even in his cups, he seemed to be aware that this was not the water closet, and he wobbled back out the door.

They did not move from under the blanket all night, and eventually, first Arya dropped off, and then drained of any remains of energy or resolve, Lottie's eyes closed. At some point in the early hours, something tiny and warm nudged Lottie's hand, but sharing the blanket with mice was the least of her worries.

She had come full circle, back to what she once ran from, doing the same kind of work for the same amount of pitiful money in the same poor conditions. Only this time she had brought Arya along with her, when the child was probably much safer with the duke and duchess, or even with Nathaniel.

Lottie did not want to live like this; it was no better than what she had run from years before. Maybe their next resting place would be better. Maybe.

***

Lottie took a risk and took Arya back to the tavern where Nathaniel had found them. They arrived early before the landlord got out of his bed. Knocking gently on the back door, the landlord's wife, Betsy, answered the door and welcomed them with a hug.

She brought them into the warm kitchen, fed them heartily while she boiled up some water, and Lottie and Arya were able to clean themselves without fear of being walked in on. Betsy rustled up a change of clothes for them both, and they felt better than they had in weeks. They could not stay there longer than a few hours, and Lottie tearfully and most gratefully accepted the few pennies that Betsy pressed into her palm as they left.

"When I was just a little older than you, Arya, my favourite thing was to go to a nicer part of the city and watch the toffs with their expensive dresses and shoes as they walked around. Would you like that?" Lottie held Arya's hand and swung their arms, so much was her mood lifted.

"A treat?" Arya asked, with a gappy smile as her two bottom teeth had recently fallen out to make way for her big teeth.

"Yes." Lottie put her hand into her pocket, to make sure the pennies were still there. "Clean streets, nice smells, pretty people."

Arya was having great fun, several hours later, listening as Lottie made up little stories about the people who walked past. The girl's stomach rumbled loudly, even though they had eaten their fill of porridge that morning.

"Are you hungry?" Lottie laughed, and Arya nodded enthusiastically.

"Stay here with the valises, and I'll go to that stall, straight ahead. Don't move, don't talk to anyone. Do you understand?"

"Yes, Miss Green," Arya crooned.

Lottie walked across to the stall with a variety of bread and pastry items, checking over her shoulder when she arrived.

The stall-holder engaged Lottie in conversation, and it was a few minutes before she could politely pay for the goods and go back to Arya. The street was busy, and it was only when the crowd cleared, that she saw Arya was not with the valises.

Looking desperately, her head turning from side to side, Lottie's heart pounded in her chest, her throat tightening with panic.

"Arya, Arya," she called loudly, over the bustle of the street.

Could one of Nathaniel's spies have found them, or Nathaniel himself? Lottie grabbed the valises, reluctant to go too far, in case Arya returned, also so untrusting in others, that their belongings would not be taken.

Lottie climbed nearby steps for a better view of the immediate area, and after some searching, she saw a young girl in front of an expensive shop front, with her face pressed up against the glass.

She immediately headed there and found two very well-dressed, familiar-looking ladies, one of whom was talking to Arya.

"There you are; you scared me half to death, Dottie," Lottie said as she approached to give Arya a warning. They had agreed they would be Lottie and Dottie, in case they were asked by someone they did not know.

"Please accept my apologies, madam," Lottie ducked her head so that she did not make eye contact with either young woman, one of whom she recognised as Miss Arabella Hayes. "My sister knows better than to make a pest of herself."

"Oh, it's no trouble at all, I assure you," the other young lady said with a smile. "Your sister has advised me as to the prettiest hat in the shop window. More so than my own sister, who is bored of hat shopping."

"Excessively so," Arabella drawled, dragging her gaze over Lottie, her lip curling. "Pray, let us go back to the nice part of town, Daniella dearest. I cannot take any more of this stench."

Arabella turned away, and Arya stuck her tongue out at her back.

"Dottie," Lottie hissed, but Daniella smiled once more.

"Please forgive my sister's manners. Your sister is but a child, mine not so." Daniella placed her hand briefly on Arya's hair.

"There you are." A man's upper-class tones filled the air. "I thought you'd been kidnapped by some ruffians."

The man laughed, along with Arabella, but Daniella smiled apologetically.

"I'm perfectly safe, Barney," she answered, softly.

Lottie had seen Miss Daniella Hayes at a ball, from a distance, and Freya had told her that she was engaged to be married to Barnaby, the Earl of Westeroy. And that Miss Arabella, two years older, was most put out at her younger sister's successful connection.

"Who are these two?" Barney inspected Lottie and Arya and was well-bred enough not to outwardly show any distaste.

Instead, he reached inside his coat pocket, drew out two coins, and gave one to Lottie and one to Arya.

"Good day to you," Barney said, linking his arm with his fiancée, and drawing her along with him.

Lottie watched them go, unsure whether to be thankful that Arabella had not recognised her or insulted that their male friend had mistaken them as beggars.

***

"What were you doing?" Lottie whispered as she pulled Arya and the two valises in the opposite direction.

"A whole shilling," Arya trilled, thrilled to have earned so much money. "You told me you used to pretend to be lost and alone when you were little. Did you ever get so much?"

Lottie wondered if being so open with Arya was so good, especially as she seemed to soak up everything she told her.

"No, I never did," Lottie confessed, feeling cheap and belittled, even though they had enough money to rent a decent room for a week or two if they were careful.

They slept well and ate well, and then as quickly as they got it, it was spent, and they were back on their bones.

Arya became a little belligerent, having been spoiled for a while. Her sunny nature disappeared behind a cloud, and she sulked for hours on end when Lottie had to refuse her as they passed by a market stall with sweets.

Lottie was upset because this was all of her doing, and tried to think of a way that would not result in her going cap in hand to

Nathaniel to beg for his patronage. Other options would be Lady Anne or Freya, but she felt the former would dismiss her out of hand, and the latter would undoubtedly notify Nathaniel at once. She would rather starve herself, but she had to consider Arya's needs more than her own.

There was only one other plausible option, and so spending a precious ha'penny on a sheet of paper, an envelope, and a stamp, she wrote a letter with the stub of a pencil to ask Sir Anthony Holden for help.

***

An answer came courtesy of the landlord's wife, whom Lottie and Arya visited in case of a reply. On their third visit in a week, she pulled an envelope from inside of her dress but did not welcome them in.

"You better skedaddle, Lottie girl, his nibs has been back offering money, and after my husband lost at cards last night, he would hand you over soon as look at you."

"Thank you, Bet," Lottie whispered, opening the envelope as she collected Arya on the way out.

Sir Anthony's solution to Lottie's problem was an offer of marriage, where she and Arya and the Ringwood Manor staff could join him in Norfolk and live comfortably under his protection. He wished to know her answer, so would arrange for a representative to attend at a named location two days hence.

Lottie held Sir Anthony in warm regard because of the courtesy he extended her both while she masqueraded as Amelia and even now, knowing the circumstances in which she found herself. However, she could not, in all good conscience, marry the man and would not provide her final answer to his representative but would travel to Norfolk and tell the gentleman to his face.

The journey to the bandstand in Hyde Park started at dawn for Lottie and Arya, and they arrived in good time to meet Sir Anthony's representative. Arya was tired from their almost five-mile walk and had fallen asleep on the steps of the bandstand. Lottie expected a manservant in lieu of his master and was surprised indeed to see Lady Anne arrive in a carriage.

She dropped the window, clearly having no intention of disembarking.

"My lady," Lottie curtsied deeply, her cheeks turning pink.

"I will not beat around the bush, my girl. Under no circumstances are you to marry Sir Holden. I forbid it," the woman intoned, like a preacher in a pulpit.

Lottie's chin lifted, she no longer needed to acquiesce to Lady Anne's demands.

"The gentleman has made me a generous offer, Lady Anne. I would be foolish to refuse it."

Lady Anne's eyes slid to the sleeping Arya, and her nostrils flared.

"I have an arrangement with a mutual acquaintance to keep all suitors away from you. Not that I need to do so since you were unmasked."

"With Lord Audley-Sinclair?" Lottie demanded, watching closely for Lady Anne's reaction. There was none other than a flare of her nostrils. "But your arrangement was with me, my Lady, to assist me in finding a suitable match."

Lottie was under no misapprehension that the woman would do whatever it took for the most gain.

"Our arrangement ended at Freshford the night you took the Lord's ward."

Lady Anne handed Lottie a pouch, which contained stationery and a pen.

"I am late for another appointment, girl. You have five minutes to write your reply, although Sir Anthony will know your answer when I return alone."

Lottie wrote a gentle refusal, telling Sir Holden that she was not good enough for him, and she should not have presumed upon his kindness. She hoped he would save face after going to so much effort to send Lady Anne to find out her answer.

She sealed the envelope and handed it and the pouch back to Lady Anne.

"I suggest you send that child back to its rightful owner, young lady, or the truth will come out."

Lottie watched the carriage depart and thought on the arrangement Lady Anne had with Nathaniel. He had inadvertently ruined her only chance to give Arya the upbringing she deserved, just like he had ruined Amelia's future.

Yes, he was the one she should blame, for this was not only of her own doing. The unravelling story had started before she knew of Amelia, Lord Audley-Sinclair, and their daughter, Arya.

Chapter 19

"Lord Audley-Sinclair." Nathaniel heard the breathy whisper at the same time he felt the silk of a woman's dress brush his hand.

Looking up from his study of the ruby red wine in its fine Waterford crystal glass, Nathaniel found himself practically toe to toe with Miss Arabella Hayes. Propriety did not allow for conversation between the two of them, and he wondered at her bold approach.

This was the type of behaviour he had been so partial to, pushing aside societal rules and flouting the norm. He was no longer inclined, or at least, nowhere near as much, since Arya had disappeared from his life.

Glancing past the young lady, Nathaniel could see Barney and Miss Daniella Hayes fast approaching. Miss Arabella was not as brazen as she pretended, simply trying hard to be something she was not.

The thought brought Lottie to the forefront of Nathaniel's mind, and on nights like this, at glittering balls such as these, he still looked for her. He did not see Arabella standing right in front of him.

"My Lord," a kind, friendly voice echoed that of her sister, and Barney's fiancée held her hand out with a smile by way of greeting.

Arabella moved to the side, as required, and waited to be introduced by her younger, engaged sister.

"Miss Hayes, such a pleasure. My friend, the Earl of Westeroy, looks happier and more content at each meeting."

Nathaniel took Daniella's hand and kissed the back of her glove, before bowing to Barney.

"And you look glummer and more morose at each meeting, Audley-Sinclair." Barney beamed, slapping his friend on the back. "You know Miss Arabella Hayes, of course."

Arabella sent a thankful look toward her future brother-in-law and then curtsied deeply, holding the pose for a moment longer than necessary, making sure his Lordship had a good look at her wares without any question.

"Good evening, Miss Hayes." Nathaniel gave a little bow but turned his attention to Barney and his beloved.

"What do I have to be glum about, Westeroy, with such lovely company this evening," Nathaniel deflected, but he caught Daniella looking at him with concern.

"I do believe some woman has finally broken that hard heart of yours, my friend. It was bound to happen one of these days. Once they catch you, you're in trouble." Barney clutched his heart and rolled his eyes, and Daniella smiled, rapping her fan gently on her fiancé's knuckles.

"A broken heart is no laughing matter, your Grace," she chided him.

"I know exactly the cure for such an ailment, my Lord," Arabella cooed, as she moved closer to him, linking her arm with his. "Dance with me, and I'll tell you just how I plan to fix you, sir."

Daniella gasped a little and exchanged a look with Barney, who smiled broadly.

"Capital idea, Miss Hayes," Barney said. "My dear, shall we take up our positions?"

"Your Grace, the dancers have not yet completed their set. We must be patient."

Nathaniel shook his head; sometimes Barney was like a huge puppy, overexcitable and in need of a good walk or, in this instance, a good dance.

"Thank you for your kindness, Miss Hayes. I am not in need of fixing, I assure you, however, I do not plan to dance with any lady this evening."

Stopping just shy of stamping her heeled foot, Arabella scoffed and crossed her arms across her chest like a petulant child.

"If you're still mooning over that imposter posing as Amelia Colton, we saw a dirty servant girl begging with her young sister in Covent Garden who looked very much like her," Arabella said spitefully.

Nathaniel, who had not heard any whispers about Lottie's whereabouts for some time, grasped onto the suggestion. He faced Arabella and put his hands on her upper arms, turning her to him.

"What did you say?"

"Unhand me, sir, you're hurting me," Arabella pouted.

"Tell me exactly when and where you saw the girl and her sister, Miss Hayes." Nathaniel's desire to know made his voice low, almost menacing, and he shook her unintentionally hard.

Arabella burst into noisy tears, and Nathaniel dropped his hands from her and uttered his apologies before leaving his company standing, looking after him in confusion.

Nathaniel grabbed another glass of wine from a passing waiter and drained it in one go. He scoured around for another waiter and, instead, caught the eye of a very smug-looking Lady Anne on the arm of a very pleased-looking Sir Anthony Holden. The pair headed directly for him before he could find an escape.

"My Lord, it's been too long," Lady Anne said pleasantly and curtsied.

"Sir Holden, Lady Anne, are you well?" Nathaniel bowed, wondering why the two of them smiled so broadly like they knew a secret that nobody else knew.

"We are exceptionally well, sir," the gentleman responded. "We are recently wed, and my Lady has made me the happiest man in all of England, I am sure of it."

Nathaniel kept his eyebrows in place as he offered his congratulations and listened with increasing amazement as their story unfolded.

"To think I considered marrying Miss Charlotte Green—" Sir Holden leaned in closer to whisper. "The young lady who pretended to be Miss Amelia Colton. She wrote to me to ask for my assistance. Ever the gentleman, I made her an offer of marriage, and she turned me down very sweetly, but nonetheless, the sting was sharp."

"My husband has the most sensitive of hearts, Lord Audley-Sinclair," Lady Anne informed Nathaniel, and he wondered if her new husband knew of his wife's part in Lottie's masquerade.

"I spitefully wrote back to the girl, withdrawing the offer regardless of her refusal. In hindsight, I should be eternally grateful, as it led to this wonderful union with Lady Anne. I regret my peevish, rather ungentlemanly behaviour toward Miss Green. If I were to encounter her once more, I would wish her good health and fortune and hope she could be as happy as I."

Nathaniel had no words as Sir Holden and Lady Anne bid him farewell, heading for the dance floor. Barney and Daniella joined the line-up, and Miss Arabella, suitably recovered, had also found a partner to dance with. Usually, Nathaniel would be there with a beauty and plenty waiting in the wings for his attention, but they were not in his thoughts.

Listening to two different encounters with Lottie and Arya sent a chill of realisation along his spine. Two versions of Lottie's truth, one where she and Arya begged for money and the other where desperation drove her to ask help from a relative stranger rather than coming to him, the person who loved Arya more than anyone in the world.

Nathaniel, the memory of his actions with Miss Arabella Hayes fresh in his mind, knew he had fed into the ruin of Lottie's reputation when she was pretending to be Amelia by behaving the way he did when he first knew her in society. He treated her with contempt, disrespect, and without any sense of propriety, which should have been below him. He was supposed to be a gentleman, a Lord, and yet his disregard for the rules did not mean he could treat another person without care and consideration.

Lottie had called him out on his behaviour towards Arya and Amelia, but she had not concerned herself with his behaviour towards her.

Nathaniel needed to prove to Lottie that he cared for Arya like a daughter, that he loved her beyond anything else. He needed to show her that he took his responsibilities seriously, just as seriously as she took hers, in protecting Arya, no matter how misguided her decisions might be.

He cared for Lottie too, more than he had realised until this evening. Watching the dancers, the couples who moved together to achieve a well-rehearsed routine, he thought about how much he wanted that with Lottie, together with Arya.

Sometime later, as the guests were leaving, Sir Holden and Lady Anne stopped to say goodbye to Nathaniel.

"My Lord, I have been lucky to find love unexpectedly, but most welcome." Lady Anne looked at her husband, and Nathaniel felt she was a changed character, softened by her gentle husband. "If I can help you to find Lottie and your ward, I will do so wholeheartedly. I need to right some of my own wrongs in this matter."

Nathaniel thanked them sincerely and knew that if Lady Anne could reform her character, he could too. His actions towards Lottie and Arya needed to match his words. He needed to keep his promise to Amelia, that he would do right by her daughter. That he would do right by the woman who had turned his world upside down.

Chapter 20

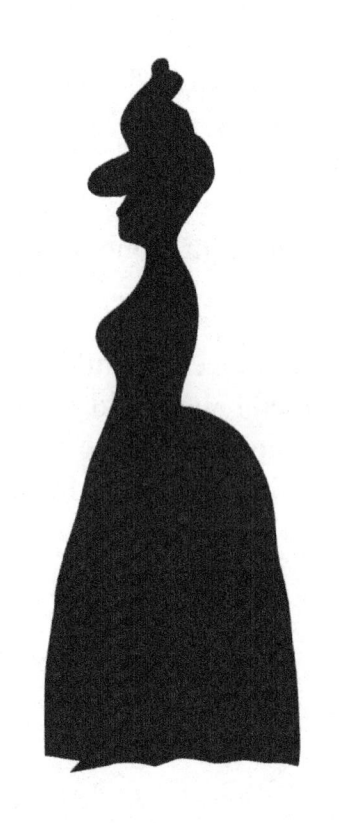

"Lottie, Lottie, can we keep him?"

Lottie, sweeping the stairs at the back of the chapel, looked up to see Arya running in circles with a small puppy chasing at her heels, barking sharply.

As Arya laughed, stopping to change direction, the dog following her faithfully already, Lottie already knew what her answer was going to be.

The little girl had immediately settled into their new accommodation, two small rooms above the stables in the courtyard that Lottie was about to sweep now. The vicar had seen her desperation the night he found them asleep in the second-to-last pew in his chapel and had offered her work and Arya an opportunity to learn with other children from the congregation in his wife's classroom.

Arya flourished, and Lottie took great pleasure in watching her grow and blossom. The vicar's wife was a very good cook, almost good enough to give Maggie a run for her money, and with nutritious fare the little girl grew stronger and taller.

"You must ask the Reverend and Mrs. Thompson."

They would say yes to Arya's request without hesitation, with her beguiling smile and pleading eyes. With no children of their own, they doted on the girl, and both she and Arya held them in the highest esteem. Without anyone else to care for them, to help them and guide them, the Thompsons were more family to her than her own mother and Arya's father. Lottie knew that love existed; she had seen it before with Holmes and Maggie and, in a way, Lady Eleanor, who had taken her into her home.

To experience it as an adult with her own responsibilities, helped Lottie begin to heal some of her own hurts from the past, just as Arya was flourishing even though she had been ripped from everything she knew.

Lottie, almost at breaking point when she came to the chapel that night, had learned that there was no point in pretending any longer, the truth would always find a way to come out. She had poured her heart out, and more, to Mrs. Thompson that evening, as the kindly woman brought Lottie and Arya to their small dwelling adjoining the chapel. As Arya slept on the floor in front of the fire, Lottie had told everything, from her own childhood, running away, being brought to Ringwood Manor, and everything thereafter.

Mrs. Thompson had commiserated how horrible it must have been when Lottie's secret was spewed forth by Sir Shepherd. Lottie had confessed herself glad that both Amelia and Lady Eleanor were not alive to witness the scandal. What Amelia had started when she eloped with Sir Shepherd, Lottie herself had ended, and she had to make the best of her situation for Arya's sake.

It was a topic that Lottie revisited often in her own mind, and that Saturday afternoon, as they took afternoon tea with the Reverend and Mrs. Thompson, the adults talked in quiet voices, given the subject of their discussion.

Arya rolled on the parlour floor with the puppy she had named George.

"Have you given your future any more thought, my dear?" The Reverend smiled at Arya's high jinx. "You are, of course, welcome to stay here for as long as you wish, but I have a feeling, even in this quiet corner of Blackfriars, the Lord will find you."

Lottie exchanged a look with Mrs. Thompson, both familiar with his dry sense of humour. He was fond of trying to bring Lottie into the religious fold, but on this occasion, she would assume he was talking about Nathaniel.

"I dream of bringing Arya to Ringwood Manor to live in the home that is rightly hers as heir to the Gilroy estate. But I dare not return because Lord Audrey-Sinclair's spies are no doubt everywhere. She is my world, and I will never forsake her, but it is time I right the wrongs I have brought upon Arya."

"Where to start?" Mrs. Thompson asked, squeezing Lottie's hand.

"Back at the beginning, where it all started."

***

On Monday morning, after Arya had started her lessons, Lottie finished her duties and headed for the city offices of Lightfoot and Geary Solicitors to make an appointment with Mr. Forbes.

"Good day," Lottie clutched her purse in front of her as if it were a shield and she were going to battle. "Might I enquire when Mr. Forbes will next be in attendance in your London office, sir?"

She sounded young, her voice small in the high-ceilinged office, where at least ten men sat behind big oak desks, and all at once, they turned their attention to her.

"Forbes?" The old man who stood to greet her upon her entrance looked over his half-moon spectacles. "Forbes?"

"From your Winchester office. He oversaw the inheritance of the late Lady Eleanor Gilroy's estate."

"Your name, madam?"

Lottie wanted no more of the lies and pretence, but she doubted her real name would carry any clout here.

"Miss Amelia Colt—."

"Miss Colton is Lady Gilroy's niece, Mr. Geary," a familiar voice floated downwards as a gentleman trotted down the stairs as fast as was decent. "A pleasure to see you again, madam."

Mr. Forbes approached with a smile and bowed deeply.

"Sir, I am very glad to find you here in London," Lottie said with relief, for at least one individual still believed her charade.

"How can we be of service, Miss Colton?" Mr. Geary bowed stiffly, as he spoke.

"I have a matter of high sensitivity to discuss with Mr. Forbes, given his understanding of my circumstances," Lottie said kindly and allowed the younger man to lead her to a private area at the back of the office.

"Tell me how I can help, madam."

Lottie opened her purse and brought out a letter, which she gave to him. Therein, she gave a full and frank account of her misdemeanours, and how she came to be in London, instead of at Ringwood Manor.

Forbes read the letter in silence, referring back to earlier passages as if checking the facts, and then he folded the paper and handed it back to Lottie.

"Miss Green, do I understand correctly?" Forbes dropped his voice as he leaned closer. "That you are renouncing any claim to the Gilroy inheritance?"

"Yes, sir," Lottie said in a rush of breath. "Miss Arya is the true heir, and it is imperative that the estate is correctly inherited by Miss Amelia Colton's only daughter."

Forbes stroked his chin while he considered the request.

"The child's father?"

"I can only say with certainty that Lord Nathaniel Audley-Sinclair is Arya's guardian. I have no proof either way, but she has been under his guardianship, as far as I can gather, since her mother's untimely death."

Lottie wanted only to deal with the truth, but she had only her assumptions to go on, which would not stand up in a courtroom.

"If such a connection is established, his Lordship should manage Miss Arya's affairs, her upbringing, and the estate in trust, until the young lady reaches her majority or is married. Where will this leave you, Miss Green?"

Lottie had considered this very question, but all she knew was that she could, no, would never abandon Arya. Not that Amelia had abandoned her daughter, as she had died in childbirth. But Lottie's own mother begot her, gave up on her, and left her to fend for herself as a child.

Lottie would always put Arya first, but what that would mean in real terms was as yet unknown.

"Mr. Forbes, I will accept whatever conditions Lord Audley-Sinclair may set on me, as long as I am part of Arya's world."

For all the gravity of the situation, Lottie pondered whether Nathaniel would welcome Arya's dog as warmly as he would its young mistress.

***

Old habits died hard, and Nathaniel showed the woman, whose name he could not recall or had never bothered to ask for, out of the tradesmen's door before the late November sun had fully risen.

Before Arya was taken from his life, he would always ensure he left his lovers' abodes to be home before the little girl awoke, entering quietly through the tradesmen's door. He never brought a woman to him when he was in residence at the Windsor house, as that was Arya's sanctuary.

But since she had been gone, he had not travelled out of the country in case Arya returned, and he needed to get back to her. Her bedclothes were freshly laundered every week and her governess and the full household staff remained active and in situ, just in case.

As he climbed up the stairs to his chambers, his limbs like lead, his heart heavy, the doorbell sounded, pealing sharply through his whiskey-fogged brain.

"Taylor, get rid of the." Nathaniel leaned over the banister and shouted down to the ground floor.

The butler appeared instantly, looked up, and nodded his assent.

Nathaniel had every intention of lounging in his undershirt, sipping more whiskey until the bath his manservant should be drawing him was ready. And then more whiskey until he passed out. At least then, the pain would hurt less.

Shrugging his coat onto the chaise, Nathaniel brooded out of the window, his head throbbing, and it took a while for the sounds of a child's voice to filter through his hangover and almost perpetual bad mood. He was hearing things, clearly, and that made him crosser. He slugged back the alcohol and poured another.

He missed Arya dreadfully, used to her being there, even though he was hardly home during those first six years of her life. He had missed out on so much because of his work and his philandering ways, and now he was paying the price.

By the time his bath was drawn, his thoughts, as usual, wandered towards the less salubrious parts of London, to wherever Lottie and Arya lived. Just miles apart but a world away. Each time he thought he got near, they had moved. For his own sanity, he told his network that he only wanted to know when there had been a positive sighting of the pair. For every negative report, another tiny part of his already cracking heart crumbled to dust.

Just yesterday, he heard through his contacts that Lottie had been seen making enquiries at a solicitor's office, Lightfoot and Geary. Nathaniel recognised the name; the solicitor had been present at the funeral of Lady Eleanor, but he could not believe that Lottie could afford any legal services, let alone those of a very well-established, fourth-generation business.

Nathaniel heard the child's laughter again, followed by the thundering of footsteps.

He stomped across the room, pulled open the door, fully prepared to take his frustration and anger out on whichever servant was making the noise, only to have the wind knocked from his body as a small force collided with him.

Looking down, barely believing what his eyes were telling him, there was Arya, her arms wrapped around his waist. Her eyes were closed, her lips curled in a smile, and she sighed happily.

His heart in his throat, he pressed his palm to the top of her head, closing his eyes with utter relief. He heard footsteps and the scrabbling of claws on the wooden stairs.

He opened his eyes to see who had accompanied Arya and saw Lottie taking the next set of stairs, stopping two steps up. She turned and met his gaze. A dog appeared at the top of the stairs and ran straight for Arya.

"Now I'm home, George will need somewhere to sleep, as we left his bed at the chapel." Arya picked the dog up, rattling off instructions, like pellets from a pistol. "Miss Lottie will be my governess, and we can all be together. Apart from second Saturdays, when we'll have afternoon tea with the Reverend and Mrs. Thompson."

"Welcome home, Arya," Nathaniel told her softly.

Arya ran past Lottie, up the two flights of stairs to her playroom, and before long, he heard the excited tones of the household staff as they greeted her.

Nathaniel turned his gaze to Lottie, silent tension simmering between them for a long moment. He knew he should send her packing with a flea in her ear for what she had put him and Arya through. But he could not find any words because she looked more beautiful than he remembered in all her guises: grieving for Lady Eleanor, dancing with her at the grandest balls in London and Bath, kissing her in the backstreets of Bloomsbury, proposing to her in a tavern in the slums of Cheapside.

"We have much to discuss, Miss Green. Please." Nathaniel moved to stand at the top of the stairs and held his hand out. "Join me in my study."

She followed him down and entered the study, looking around her, as he closed the door behind her.

"Pray be seated," he said, as he rounded the desk, but she remained standing.

"If I may get to the crux of the matter, my Lord," Lottie began, and for the first time, he noticed the manila folder she carried under her arm, which she was now opening. "I have renounced any claim to the Gilroy estate, and it has been legally transferred to Miss Arya Colt—, Miss Arya Audley-Sinclair. To be held in trust, by yourself as her legal guardian, until she comes of age or is married, whichever comes first."

Nathaniel's eyebrows rose in surprise at the conjoining of his surname with Arya. He remembered Lottie's evaluation of his parental responsibilities and his treatment of Amelia upon learning she was pregnant. At the time, he had not given it any further thought until now.

"The terms of this agreement include an addendum." Lottie bent forward and pushed the folder across the desk and waited as Nathaniel turned the pages, reading quickly.

"Miss Charlotte Green will become Miss Audley-Sinclair's appointed governess until such time she comes of age or marries, whichever comes first. Miss Green will work with Lord Audley-Sinclair as legal guardian to ensure Miss Audley-Sinclair's safekeeping," Nathaniel intoned, laying the document on the desk.

"Do you have questions, my Lord, about my terms?" Lottie clasped her hands behind her back, her eyes anxious, her teeth biting gently on her bottom lip.

"This document is invalid, Miss Green." Nathaniel studied her closely, as he tapped his forefinger on the paper.

"Oh?" Lottie's voice wobbled a little, and Nathaniel knew how much courage this must have taken for her to bring Arya back to him.

"Firstly, Arya already has a governess, Mrs. O'Hara, who has worked for my family since I was a small child. She has a wealth of experience in educating Arya up until her disappearance." His voice was pleasant enough, but Lottie's composure was slipping.

"Secondly, there is a factual inaccuracy herein. Arya's surname is Colton, named for her mother, not her useless waste of space of a father." Lottie's eyes widened, her lips parting as she gasped.

"Finally, your terms do not mention a price, Miss Green, what you expect in return for giving up your life for the next eleven or so years until Arya reaches her majority."

Tears filled her eyes and hovered on her lashes. Nathaniel felt bad, for his intention was not to break her down, to belittle her in any way. He wanted badly to take Lottie in his arms, to hold her close, to apologise for his part in her downfall. But he needed first to regain her trust.

"Your terms are agreeable, Miss Green; however, let us rewrite this agreement and have your solicitor at Lightfoot and Geary notarise it."

Nathaniel stood, and Lottie watched him with bated breath, her heartbeat almost palpable in the room.

"I propose you act as Arya's companion, offering the support and comfort she needs. You will, of course, live here or take advantage of any of my homes as you see fit for Arya's needs. All expenses will be taken care of, and you will enjoy an allowance for Arya's clothing and accoutrements, as well as your own. Your man, Holmes, and his wife are welcome to join our household, if they so wish, until such time Arya can make her own decisions about Ringwood Manor, her familial home. Mrs. O'Hara will support you with Arya's education. You and I, Miss Green, will consult on decisions about Arya's future. What say you?"

"I agree, Lord Audley-Sinclair. Your revised terms are most agreeable."

Nathaniel rounded his desk and stood before Lottie. She looked up at him, her eyes shining, her cheeks glowing, and he was thankful that she had accepted at least one of his proposals.

As they shook hands to seal the deal, he felt the warmth of her hand through her glove. He was heartily sure he had the best end of their agreement. Not only did he have Arya back, but he also had Lottie, and a chance to prove his worth to her.

To win her trust. To win her heart. To win her love.

Chapter 21

Lottie stretched luxuriantly, not quite ready to be fully awake and ready before Arya knocked at her door like she did every morning, and snuggled with her for a few moments.

Mrs. O'Hara, the governess, did not approve of this informality, but she turned a blind eye because she knew how much Arya had benefitted from being loved.

Although Lottie had experienced luxury when she took on the mantle of Amelia, this time round, as herself, she appreciated it all the more, especially after living hand to mouth for months with Arya.

As the little girl knocked, entered, and dove under the sheets before Lottie had even said come in, it was hard to believe that their adventures, as Arya called them, had no lasting effect on her. If anything, the exposure to a world outside of the lovely house in Windsor where she had lived for her whole life had made her a little wise—street-wise—beyond her seven years.

"What do you want to do today after your lessons with Mrs. O'Hara? A walk in the park, a visit to the shops?"

"May we watch for toffs?" Arya asked, and Lottie hid her smile.

This was what she had nicknamed her favourite hobby as a child, and it had resonated with Arya.

The girl did not know that she was a toff. She did not see herself any differently from the girl who had slept in real hovels and gone hungry for days on end. Now, she had the best of everything, the nicest clothes, more food than she ever needed, and plenty of love to boot.

"Yes, my love, we can toff watch," Lottie replied, willing to do anything she could to make Arya happy.

***

Lottie's ideas about Nathaniel were changing, as she saw him from a different perspective. He was in the country for the majority of the time, and she knew from Mrs. O'Hara, that had started when Arya went away.

"This house is starting to feel like a home, like the one the Lord and his brother grew up in," the governess told Lottie as she collected Arya from her lessons later that morning. "I thought the child would be good for his Lordship but having you here as Arya's companion has done wonders for his disposition, Miss Green."

Nathaniel played with Arya nearly every day, if his business was completed in time, and Lottie's relationship with him shifted. Although she would never dream of ever telling him, she was falling in love with him a little more every day. At home, he was all the man she could ever want, kind, thoughtful, sensitive to her needs. All the man she could ever want but would never have.

With her role as Arya's companion, they could be seen out in public now without any impropriety. Although of late, as her affection grew, she thought time and again of how it felt to be kissed by Nathaniel.

Their evening meal together that evening, after Arya was in bed, was one such occasion where she studied Nathaniel for an overtly long moment. He caught her gaze, and she felt her cheeks flush with warmth.

"Are you well, Miss Green?" Nathaniel laid down his cutlery, swallowed, and wiped the corners of his mouth with the white linen napkin, drawing her attention.

"I fear I am sat too close to the fire, my Lord." Lottie lowered her gaze.

It simply would not do to fawn over the gentleman.

However, she could not help but watch him as he stood and held her gaze. Moving closer to her, he bowed and held out his hand.

"Let us retire to the sitting room, Lottie."

While she had called him Nathaniel in her mind for a long time, to hear him call her Lottie felt incredibly intimate.

"Thank you, sir."

Lottie took his hand and let him lead her through to his formal sitting room, as was his habit after their meal, but this felt different. He led her to the chaise, as normal, but instead of taking a chair, he sat down next to her.

Her heart began to beat faster as he relaxed somewhat, talking about his day, sharing some insights into the nature of his business. This was a change in their relationship, the balance moving more towards the centre of the scale, moving from employer and employee to man and woman.

"I look forward to this part of my day more and more, Lottie. I trust you implicitly with Arya, and I believe you are as honest as the day is long. Can I trust you with the truth?"

Lottie was thrilled to know that his opinion of her had changed, but also a little worried about what he might tell her. There was nothing else she had to confess about herself, so was it about Arya or himself?

"Of course, my Lord."

"You once told me I shirked my parental responsibilities towards Arya. You also assumed the child should have my surname. While I admit to not paying as much attention to the child as I should, I am making amends for that oversight."

She nodded in agreement.

"I am not Arya's father, which is why her surname is Colton. Amelia made a very poor choice in becoming attached to the man in the first instance, and when he let her down, I stepped in out of respect for my mother's friendship with Lady Eleanor."

Lottie felt her eyes growing wide.

"Sir, I apologise for the incorrect assumption. When I read Amelia's letters, after Lady Eleanor's death, I felt very strongly that the gentleman who broke her heart should be exposed. The day you came to visit me at Ringwood, I had just discovered your name in Amelia's letter and came to the wrong conclusion, I see that now."

"I accept your apology, my dear. But I should extend you the same courtesy. When I learned the identity of the man who you suspected of paying an overt interest in the child, the man you had seen waiting outside the nursery at Freshford, I was convinced you had only Arya's best interests at heart. Even if your actions were a little extreme."

Lottie thought for a moment about the truth Nathaniel had shared with her. It had puzzled her why Sir Shepherd had paid so much attention to a child, to Arya, but had not given it any further thought once she had taken Arya from Bath, then to Winchester, then to London.

"Is Sir Anthony Shepherd Arya's father? Is he the man who broke Amelia's heart?"

***

After the revelation of the evening, Lottie retired and, sitting at her own desk, read all of Amelia's letters again by candlelight. With the truth now known, Lottie felt more connected to all the characters in Amelia's story. The heroine, Amelia Colton, the villain, Sir Shepherd, and the hero, Lord Nathaniel Audley-Sinclair. What part might Lady Eleanor have played if she had read the letters from her niece? Would the story have turned out differently?

Lottie took out a sheet of paper, dipped her pen in the inkwell, and started her own letter to Lady Eleanor. A letter that she would never send, just like Amelia's were never read. She would add her own chapters to the ongoing saga.

Arya, when she was old enough or curious enough to learn about her mother and her great-aunt, could read the story that started with Amelia and continued with Arya.

***

Several weeks later, Nathaniel had business in Bath and asked Lottie and Arya if they would like to pay a visit to Freshford at the invitation of the duke and duchess. Arya was beside herself with excitement to see Marie, Michaela, and Missy and talked incessantly all the way from London to Newbury before she fell asleep.

Nathaniel and Lottie exchanged a smile, both glad of the silence, but Lottie's eyes slid away before he could see her thoughts. As they became closer, Nathaniel was exceptionally perceptive about Lottie's emotions and could often tell if she was worried or upset. Today was no different.

He reached across the carriage and took Lottie's hand.

"Do you have something on your mind, Lottie?" His voice was warm, and Lottie's eyes shone with tears.

His kindness was most endearing, and she had to be careful that her love for him did not reveal itself.

"I confess to feeling nervous to see their Graces once more. It feels like a lifetime ago that I ran from Freshford with Arya. You had entrusted Arya's care to them, and I have no doubt that I caused much embarrassment, especially after Sir Shepherd's revelation."

Nathaniel's hand squeezed hers, and she had an overwhelming need to feel the comfort of his arms around her.

The last time she visited Freshford, under the guise of Miss Amelia Colton, Freya had treated her as a true friend. Returning as Miss Lottie Green, former servant, was a different matter.

"Perhaps you should trust in the duchess' good judgement, Lottie, before making any assumptions."

He smiled gently, his touch and his words reassuring, and Lottie trusted his advice. He no longer had any ulterior motives. He knew everything about her, and she had no need to hide. She could be her true self. That was all she needed to be.

When they arrived at Freshford, they were welcomed warmly, and Arya was stolen away by the three girls to play as quickly as Nathaniel was spirited away by the duke to talk about politics and hunting.

Freya and Lottie were left alone, and Lottie curtsied deeply.

"Your Grace, I beg for your forgiveness for the deceitful start to our friend—" she faltered, and Freya stepped forward and embraced her.

"We never stopped being friends, Lottie, if I may call you so?" Freya looked a little shy, and Lottie was reassured.

"Of course, your Grace."

Freya linked arms with her, just like she had last time as if nothing had ever happened.

"You know, I knew you were not Amelia, the moment we were introduced." They walked to Freya's sitting room, where a maid waited to serve afternoon tea.

Lottie took a seat next to her friend. "How did I give myself away?"

"Amelia and I were with child at the same time, and we connected briefly, for just a few months in London. She was shy, quiet, unassuming, and although we were the same age, she seemed so much younger. You were so alive, your eyes took in everything, you soaked up information, and looked nothing like Amelia."

"I wonder that other people of Amelia's acquaintance did not realise I was not she," Lottie pondered. "Miss Arabella Hayes, I believed, made a connection when she questioned me about my language skills."

"Indeed," Freya eyed Lottie over her cup of tea. "And who should come to your aid, but Lord Audley-Sinclair? Not that you needed saving. Your Italian was quite beautiful. Besides, Miss Hayes had her nose put out of joint by the attention the Lord was paying you, rather than her."

"I did not encourage it." Lottie smiled.

"And yet, he is quite enamoured of you, my dear. It is writ clear on the man's face, in his eyes."

Lottie sipped her tea and was secretly delighted that it was obvious to others, for she had supposed she was imagining his affection. She knew they were the most unlikely match; she was not high-born, had no dowry, nor title, but perhaps her love would suffice?

***

Lottie peered out of the study window where she had a view of both ends of the street, in Windsor. The rain fell in sheets, the thunder rattled the panes of glass in their frames, and she could not sleep for worrying.

Nathaniel had sent word that he would be home that morning, and now, over twelve hours had passed, and he had not yet returned.

She not only worried about Arya's safety but now also Nathaniel's, given the information he had shared with her about his dangerous and secret missions for important people in government and in the court.

Lottie missed him when he was gone, usually for one or two days at a time. This time he had been gone for the best part of a month, travelling to the continent, and she was more eager than ever for his return.

Lightning illuminated the street, and Lottie strained to see if there was anyone about. She could see no one.

Panic set in as she heard the rattle of a door handle and realised it came from the tradesmen's door at the back of the house. Nathaniel told her to always lock it at dusk, but she realised now, if it was him, he had no way of gaining entry.

Running down the stairs, her robe flying behind her, Lottie rushed to the back door, unlocked it, and threw it open without hesitation.

"My Lord, welcome home," she said and pulled him inside, uncaring of the water cascading from his hat and raincoat.

"Lottie, what if I'd been a burglar or worse? You'd just invite them into our home," he teased, shutting the door behind him.

"Nathaniel, I—" Lottie was about to chide him when he pulled her into his arms.

He smiled and covered her lips with his, pulling her close, and Lottie gave herself up to the pleasure of being held, kissed by the man she loved. The man she wanted to spend the rest of her life with.

Epilogue

"Is she expecting us, my Lady?" Nathaniel asked the woman on his arm, his wife, the Lady Charlotte Audley-Sinclair.

Lottie laughed. She still found it hard to believe that she was married to this man, who had once infuriated and belittled her.

"I do not believe so, my Lord. Mrs. O'Hara told Arya we would be gone all day."

They both looked over the grassy area to where Arya and her governess were partaking in a picnic lunch, and, as if the girl was aware of their perusal, she jumped up as soon as she saw them and ran toward them.

Arya stopped short, curtsied to them both, and then threw herself into Lottie's arms.

"I am happy to see you."

"We have some important matters to discuss with you, young lady. Please walk with us," Nathaniel said, a little formally.

"Yes, sir," Arya's eyes widened as she looked up at her guardian.

Lottie could tell that her husband, who had fought in many battles and travelled the world on secret missions, was nervous about talking to a seven-year-old child.

"We attended several appointments today, Arya, one with my solicitor and one with Dr. Montague," Nathan told her, and the child's hand slipped into Lottie's.

"Are you ill, my Lady?" Arya's bottom lip trembled slightly as she spoke.

Lottie had made several visits recently to the physician and had taken to her bed on several occasions with bilious attacks.

"Let us discuss the most important appointment, as it needs immediate attention from us all. The other"—Nathaniel paused, glancing at Lottie lovingly—"will be long term."

Lottie could not contain herself, sure that Nathaniel would take an age.

"Arya, we would like to adopt you so that you will become our daughter. We love you already as if you are ours, but it will officially make us a family in the eyes of the law."

Lottie bent down so that she could look into Arya's eyes.

"I can call you Mama and Papa?" Her eyes shone with tears, and she looked from Lottie to Nathaniel.

Nathaniel, a lord, dropped uncaring to his knees and pulled the little girl into his embrace.

"My darling girl, will you accept us as your parents? I promise we will love you as our own for the rest of our days, and beyond."

Lottie's eyes brimmed with tears and her heart felt so full of love, pride, and happiness, she was sure it would burst. Nathaniel's words to Arya echoed the vows he made to Lottie on their wedding day several months before.

Arya nodded her silent consent, holding onto the man who was to become her father. After a moment, she turned to Lottie and fell upon her, raining kisses on her damp cheeks.

"Does this make you happy, my darling?" Lottie asked.

"I am happier than when I got George," Arya exclaimed.

While Nathaniel looked unimpressed, as he was not overly keen on the dog that Arya brought home with her, but Lottie knew this was high praise indeed. He sought Lottie's permission with a lift of his eyebrow to share their other news. She nodded, savouring the last moment of their shared secret that gave them both so much joy.

"Arya, as our daughter, you are our only child; however, in a few months, this will change. You will be the oldest, you will be a big sister. Your mama is going to have a baby." Nathaniel's voice broke with raw emotion, and he stood, turning away slightly so they would not see the tears Lottie was sure he blinked away.

"Oh, oh, I must tell Mrs. O'Hara, she will need to teach both of us. However will she manage?" Arya jumped to her feet and ran back to her governess to deliver the news.

"She's pleased, I think," Nathaniel said with a smile, as he helped Lottie to stand. "I've been considering our future, Lottie, given the impending arrival of our baby. I will find a more suitable, less dangerous profession."

"He or she will not be here for six months or so, my love." Lottie pressed her hands against his chest. "I will not deny you anything, nor ask you to change, to be anything different than you are. You have given me the chance to be myself, to be what I always dreamed of: a wife and a mother."

"I will always put you and our children above all else. I love you, simply and purely, Lottie, my love, my life."

Lottie kissed Nathaniel, long and hard, in front of anyone who cared to see. He was her husband, she was his wife, and there was no impropriety in being in love.

The end.

Printed in Great Britain
by Amazon